FREE FALLING

BOOK 1 OF THE IRISH END GAMES

SUSAN KIERNAN-LEWIS

SAN MARCO PRESS

Free Falling. Book 1 of the Irish End Games.

Copyright 2012 by Susan Kiernan-Lewis.

Ella Out of Time
Swept Away
Carried Away
Stolen Away

1

The bad thing happened on the second day of their vacation.

Although they would end up calling it many things in the coming years—the crisis, the blackout, the incident—the event would always be defined by one important feature: In a flash, it changed everyone's lives forever.

The trip itself began with anticipation and expectation like every other vacation they had ever taken as a family. The Boeing 757 touched down at Shannon Airport outside of Limerick in early September. Sarah could feel her ten year old son's excitement in the seat next to hers.

"And you're positive I'll be able to recharge my iPhone?" he asked, as he stared out the airplane window.

"Ireland is not a third world country," his father said as he unbuckled his seatbelt. "In fact, I read that they lead the world in computer technology or something." He stood and pulled down the carry-on luggage from the overhead compartment.

"But consider giving the iPhone a break," Sarah said. "We're here to see Ireland. It's a very rural country with—"

"You told me, Mom," John said. "I get it. Rural, beautiful, lots of history and stuff. I just don't want to be bored out of my mind, okay? I mean, while you and Dad are sitting in cafés and visiting museums, I need my stuff, too."

Sarah caught her husband's eye.

He shook his head. *Plenty of time to fight this battle later*, his expression said.

"Come on, sport," he said. "Let's find some authentic Irish food. And a lager."

"Cool. They have logging in Ireland? Like in Seattle?"

Sarah laughed. "Let's go find those loggers."

That first night they stayed in a traditional Irish hotel and ate a simple meat stew. They spent three hours in the corner pub singing with other tourists and washing away their jet lag with the local brew. They tucked John into a spare bed in their small hotel room. Sarah and David kissed briefly before falling into bed exhausted.

The next morning it was raining.

"It's freezing outside," John said as he entered the hotel dining room. "And it's only September."

"Come get warm by the fire and eat something," Sarah said. "Dad's out renting the car for our drive to the village where we'll be staying."

John sat down and examined his breakfast plate.

"They cooked the tomatoes."

"They do, over here."

"And I wanted bacon but they gave me ham."

"This is what their bacon looks like."

"It's ham."

"Well, so is bacon, really."

"No, bacon and ham both come from a pig but bacon is not ham."

"Okay. But this is as close to bacon as you get for the next ten days, okay?"

"The toast is weird."

"John, everything is weird when you're in a foreign country, okay? It's part of the reason one travels. To have things not the same as where you live."

John cut a piece of ham and ate it. "It's not terrible."

"Good boy."

The door swung open and an cool blast of air invaded the room. David strode in, gave Sarah a quick kiss and sat down.

"It's really cold out there," he said, pouring himself a cup of tea. "Oh, crap. Don't they have coffee?"

"It's in the other carafe."

David tousled his son's hair. "Eating an authentic Irish breakfast, I see."

"It sucks."

"John." His mother frowned at him.

"Just kidding," he said, grinning sheepishly.

Sarah turned to David. "How long do you think it'll take us to get to Balinagh?"

"About half a day, I think," he said, pouring his coffee. "You got the directions to the rental cottage?"

"There'll be someone there to show us where everything is and to change the linens every few days, but for the most part, we'll be on our own."

"Mom? Did you ask someone about the iPhone charger?"

As THEY DROVE through the countryside, David decided Ireland was green and wet in order to stay that way. The road divided undulating hocks and hills crisscrossed by ancient stone walls. With so few trees, the green horizon seemed to stretch on indefinitely, one verdant field after another.

"Hey, there's sheep ahead." John tossed aside his Game Boy and pointed over his mother's shoulder. "Don't run over 'em, Dad."

"I won't," David said, slowing down. "But I have to admit to not knowing who has the right of way, here."

"Give it to the sheep, dear," Sarah said.

They braked to a halt.

John rolled down his window and stuck his head out.

"There's, like, a real shepherd out here and everything. And man, those sheep are dirty."

They sat in silence as the sheep and their shepherd moved slowly across the road.

As David watched the sheep, he realized that Sarah's idea to visit a remote part of Ireland was a good one. They had all gotten stretched thin with their schedules back in Jacksonville, Florida. She was probably right, too, about John's obsession with his electronics, although David had been pretty addicted to television when he was his son's age.

Even so, just being some place foreign—and rural—felt like it was already doing them all a world of good. He glanced at his wife who was frowning at the way the shepherd was handling things—as if she could will him to move his flock faster.

It was all very well for Sarah to orchestrate this vacation in order to amend what she saw as a deficit in the family (and possibly the marriage?) but he would be interested to see how *she* managed the next ten days without her smartphone, iPad and movies-on-demand.

The shepherd waved to them as he led the sheep up the hill into a pasture enclosed by a dilapidated fieldstone wall.

John pulled his head into the car. "I'm starving, Mom."

Sarah dug into her purse and handed her son a biscuit wrapped in a paper napkin.

"Here, I saved it from your breakfast."

"Oh, great. Now we're in an episode of *Survivor Man*."

"We'll stop for lunch in a bit," David said. "Want your first beer?"

"David," Sarah said, admonishingly.

John took the biscuit and bit into it. "I'm dying of thirst," he said.

BY THE TIME David parked the car in front of the little cottage, Sarah was tired and her back ached. They had stopped in Balinagh, the nearest town to the cottage, and stocked up on groceries. Because of the condition of the poor country roads, the drive had been longer than she expected.

The cottage was a one-level carriage house. It had a steep roof of shingles and a chimney between two large windows in the front. Grass lined both sides of the long drive that led from the main road to the front yard. Flowering vines crawled up the window framework and around the door which had a small porch with three flat wooden steps. A back door from the kitchen led to a courtyard of stone flanked on one side by the entrance to a small paddock with broken fence slats, a very old barn, and a vegetable garden that looked like it hadn't been tended in years.

It was clear that no one had lived here for a long time. The house was what the Irish called "self catering." Sarah didn't think it looked like it had been self-catered in a long time either.

"Wow! There's horses here. Mom, did you know there would be horses here?" John leaped out of the car and ran toward the barn.

David looked at the piece of paper Sarah held in her hand.

"Are you positive this is it?"

"David, yes. Can we, at least, look inside before you decide I've made a big mistake?"

"Did it look like this on the Internet?"

"No, this isn't..." Sarah took a breath as she felt anxiety climbing higher into her chest. "This isn't the one I saw online, remember? I got the e-mail at the airport saying that one had burned down and we were to go to this one, that it was comparable."

David stepped out of the rental car. "Did the other one have horses?"

"Of course not," she said, unhappily. "There were no horses."

"Dad! Mom! You gotta see this!" John ran back to the car. "There are three horses in there!"

"Are we supposed to take care of the horses?" David asked.

"Can we, Dad?" John jumped in delight. "Can the small one be mine?"

David looked at Sarah.

"Let's look in the house first, son," he said.

Please let it have indoor plumbing, Sarah thought as she climbed out of the car.

John ran to the front door and pushed it open. "It's not locked," he called before darting inside.

"I'm sorry, David," Sarah said. "The one I booked on the Internet was much bigger."

John met them on the porch. "It's just got one room," he said. "And only one bed. I don't get my own bed?"

Sarah and David went inside.

"Well," David said with a sigh. "To quote my son, this sucks."

A large king-sized bed was pushed up against the far wall. Next to it was a door, which Sarah hoped was to an indoor bathroom. A giant stone fireplace anchored the front wall of the house and faced the kitchen and dining area on the opposite wall. The floor was polished wood and several thick rugs covered most of it. Two easy chairs faced the fireplace.

"It's actually very cozy," David said. "Very comfy—except for the one bed thing."

"Hey! There's a TV!" John said with excitement. "On the table next to the bed." He began to fiddle with its dials.

"I wonder if they get Colbert here," David said, sitting down on the bed. "It's a nice bed."

"Look, David, I'm sorry, okay?" Sarah said. "I booked a *two-*bedroom cottage."

David looked at her. "Why don't we unpack our groceries and get settled in a little?"

"Really? You're okay with this?"

"Do we have an option?"

"I don't really know. I have a phone number."

He got up and took her in his arms. "Don't bother. I say we make the most of what we've got."

She put her head on his shoulder and felt some of the tension drain from her body.

"Thanks," she whispered.

He kissed her then called to John: "Come on, Sport. Let's unload the groceries and the luggage and Mom and I can start getting supper on the table."

"You gonna come out and see the horses?"

David looked at Sarah, who shrugged.

"Right. Okay. Show me the horses," David said. The two walked out the door and headed for the barn.

Sarah buttoned her sweater and rubbed her hands together. It was cold in the little cottage. She began looking for the thermostat she would never find.

2

It happened sometime during their first night.

They had built a fire in the fireplace and made a supper of canned stew with a fresh salad and a bottle of good South African red wine. John was able to get *Sponge Bob Square Pants* on the TV but was told he couldn't watch his first night in Ireland. The three of them bundled up in jackets and a quilt and sat outside under the stars talking and identifying constellations.

That night would be the last time that Sarah could look up to the heavens without praying. It would be the last time any of them would choose to sit outside and waste the warmth of the fireplace.

On that first night, the experiences of their day of travel and discovery had left them all ready for bed. However, the sounds of the Irish countryside, combined with the occasional horse whinny, made it difficult for both David and Sarah to fall asleep.

In the cold and foggy morning to which they awoke, they found the world forever changed.

"MOM, can we ride the horses today?"

Sarah turned in bed and put her hand out to touch her husband's shoulder.

"David," she murmured. "He shouldn't be in the barn. There are too many things to fall on his head."

"John," David groaned from his side of the bed. "Stay inside until we're all up."

"But Dad—"

"Just hang tight, John," Sarah said, groping for her iPhone on the side of the bed. Eight o'clock. "I'll make breakfast."

"Can I watch TV?" John came over and sat on the side of the bed. "Pleeeeeease?" He leaned over and kissed his mother on the cheek.

"We need to have some rules about the TV," she said.

"Thanks, Mom." He jumped up and snapped on the set.

"David. I am so not going to change one country's television laugh-track for another. It's the same droning idiocy as back home. Only the accents have changed."

David yawned and sat up beside his wife.

"Morning," he said, and kissed her.

John turned up the TV. "Mom, I think something's wrong."

"Don't tell me it doesn't work, sweetie. Because it doesn't matter anyway. We're not here to—"

David's body tensed. He jumped out of bed. "Sarah, something's happened." He stood next to his son in front of the TV set. "There's been a...an incident or something. John, go out and play."

"It's raining, Dad."

"What is it?" Sarah pulled on a sweatshirt and joined David and John in front of the TV. "What's happening?"

The images on the television looked like amateur video. There were explosions, cars flipped over, crumpled buildings, and fires. The Irish announcer alternated from a serious reporting voice to a shrillness bordering on hysteria.

"My God, what —" Sarah covered her mouth with her hands. "It's home," she turned to look at David. "It's America."

Stunned by the images, David held up a hand for silence. He listened as the newscaster intoned in a strong Irish accent: "... reports of nuclear contamination in several major cities..."

"What is it?" John looked panicked. "What's happening back home, Mom? Dad? Are we...? Are we being bombed?"

"Shhhh." Sarah wrapped her arms around her boy. "Just listen," she whispered.

"'......too soon to attribute to any specific terrorist group but certainly an attack of this magnitude..."

"My God," Sarah said and tears filled her eyes.

"Take him outside, Sarah," David said. "For God's sake, don't let him see this."

John turned to his mother. "What's happening, Mom? Is it going to be okay?"

Sarah stood and ushered the boy outside. The two of them stood on the porch. The rain splattered droplets of mud onto the legs of their pajamas. She hugged him tightly.

"It's going to be okay," she said into his hair. "It's going to be okay."

"Are they attacking us?" he asked.

"I don't know, sweetie. Dad will let us know in a bit."

AN HOUR LATER, the rain had stopped and David and Sarah sat on the front steps of the cottage. The clouds had blown away, leaving a clear blue sky. John hung on the fence of the adjoining corral talking to the horses and feeding them carrots.

"What do we do?"

David shook his head. "It's bad," he said. "They've shut down all flights in and out of the States. Indefinitely."

"So we can't get home?"

"I tried to call the American embassy in Dublin," he said, pulling out his cell phone. "But it just goes to a recording."

They were silent for a moment.

"Should we drive back to Limerick?" Sarah watched her son as he laughed while petting the forelock of the biggest horse.

"I don't know if that's a good idea. It'll be crazy there. Probably wouldn't be able to get a hotel room. At least here we have a place to stay."

"Did they say who did this to us?"

David took his wife's hand.

"They're suggesting some place in the Middle East, big surprise. They made it sound like whole cities are affected."

"Which cities?" Sarah felt the panic rise in her throat. "Washington?"

"I...I couldn't tell. It wasn't much in the way of news. It was just, you know, mayhem and fire and explosions. The Irish newscasters didn't know. Just knew the US was under attack."

All of a sudden a bright flash appeared in the sky, turning the horizon briefly white with its intensity.

"John!" David shouted. "Come to me, son!"

The boy dropped from the fence, and trotted over to where his parents sat, a questioning frown on his face in response to the panic in his father's voice.

It was over in less than five seconds. The brightness faded and the sky returned to a bright Irish fall day.

"What the hell, David? What just happened?"

"I'm not really sure."

"What was that big flash?"

"Sarah, calm down. Let's all just calm down."

"I'm scared, Dad," John said, prompting David to put his arms around him.

"Look, you guys," David said. "We're together and we're safe. That's what's important."

Sarah looked at him with fear growing in her eyes. "Something just happened *here*, didn't it?"

"I don't know, Sarah. Maybe."

She stood up. "We need to get into town and see if anybody knows anything there."

He could see she was terrified. His own heart was pounding fast in his throat. He looked out over the pasture where the flash had lit up the sky. Everything looked so normal now. So peaceful. The birds were singing.

"Sarah, let's stay calm, okay?"

"John, wanna go into town?" Sarah held out her hand to him. "Car keys, David, please."

David stood up. "I'll drive."

They all got into the small rental car, buckled up and then sat in the driveway facing the main road.

The car wouldn't start.

"Crap," David said.

Sarah looked over at him. "Do you know something?"

"I was afraid of this. The car's too new. If there's really been some kind of nuclear explosion—"

"Are you serious?" Sarah gaped at him. "Is that what you think happened? Ireland had a nuclear bomb dropped on it?"

"Mom? Dad? Is everything okay?" John's voice shook.

David opened the car door. "Let's don't do this here. Come on, sport. We're not taking the car today."

As Sarah jumped out of the car. Her purse spilled onto the dirt driveway.

"David, why is the damn car not starting?"

David ran his fingers through his hair in exasperation. "It's a world catastrophe, Sarah. If something happens to America...I mean...when *it* is in crisis, the rest of the world is affected too."

"I don't understand."

John looked from one parent to the other. "Did America get bombed?"

David turned to him and put his arm around him. "Yes, son."

"So, why doesn't our car work in Ireland?"

"That's what I would like to know, too," Sarah said, as she knelt in the dirt picking up the contents of her purse.

"Well, if *England* was bombed too—" David said.

"Did you hear on the TV that they were?"

"No, but they're our allies, and if *they* were hit, Ireland is close enough to be affected."

For a moment, no one spoke.

"That big flash that just happened," Sarah said. "Was that *Ireland* getting bombed?"

"I don't know, Sarah. Maybe."

Sarah stared at the car as if she were in a trance. "I guess this answers any question of evacuating to Limerick," she said, turning and moving slowly in the direction of the porch steps.

"Or anywhere else," David said, looking toward the dusky blue horizon.

"So, *now* do we ride?" John said brightly.

3

T he first day was the hardest.

The terror and insecurity of knowing just enough and nothing more was literally almost more than Sarah could bear.

Were their homes bombed? Was Washington still there? Were her parents alive? The frustration of no news—of not being able to *do* anything while death and destruction dismantled their country—was agony. All she could think was: *we have to do something!*

The town of Balinagh was ten miles away—too far to comfortably walk over rough and rocky Irish back roads—but there was no other way of getting there.

"Why can't we ride?" John asked for the hundredth time.

"John, please stop asking me that," Sarah said. "We don't know if these horses are used to being ridden—"

"There are saddles all over the barn."

"But if they haven't been ridden in a while," Sarah replied as patiently as she could without screaming, "they'll be too difficult for us to handle."

"Not for you," he said stubbornly.

"It's been too long since I rode a horse. I'm too rusty to be jumping on some horse I don't know."

David shrugged. "They seem gentle."

Sarah stood up from the porch step where she had been sitting.

"Both of you, listen to me. They might be gentle on the ground but hell on wheels once you're in the saddle."

"Why don't we try one out in the paddock?" David looked at his son who nodded enthusiastically.

"David, are you serious?" She looked at him with horror. "And what if one of us breaks something? Are you going to set the bone? Horses are not like golf carts, you know. They have minds of their own."

So that day they walked into town. In slightly less than four hours, they arrived tired, foot sore, blistered, and thirsty.

The first person they met was Siobhan Scahill, the village grocery store and pub owner.

"Sure, why would you be walking and you with three big horses just standing around?" she said as soon as they walked into her grocery shop which was lighted only by the daylight coming in through the big shop windows.

Sarah wanted to slap her.

"Mom says we need to take things slow," John said.

"Sure, it's slow you'll be taking things, all right," the woman said. She reached over and tousled John's hair. "But I'm sorry for your troubles. Sure, the Americans are a hard lot to take for the most part but we love 'em, God knows we do. My own lad, Mickey, lives in New Jersey."

Sarah tried not to break down crying right in the store.

"Have you heard from him?" David asked. "Or any news at all?"

The woman shook her head.

"Sure, no," she said. "Just something terrible bad, that's for sure. The telly went out about two hours ago with the rest of the power." She indicated the dark overhead light fixtures. "My Mickey is hard to locate at the best of times. If I don't hear from him in another few weeks, then I'll start to worry." She nodded to the shelves in her store. "People have already come to stock up and I don't expect much in the way of deliveries, now do I? What took you so long to come to town?"

"We woulda driven," John said. "But our car won't start."

"No, nor anybody else's," Siobhan said. "Although Jimmy Hennessey did say he got his tractor to working."

"You've got nothing at all?" David asked, looking about the store. "No milk, no cans of stuff?"

"Sorry, no," she shook her head. "I'm dead cleaned out. But you're staying at the McKinney place, aren't you?"

"McGutherie," Sarah said.

"McGutherie's burned down last year," Siobhan said. "I'm sure it's the McKinney place you're at now. It's more of a weekend cabin, not really a tourist rental, aye?"

"That explains a lot."

"But you've got the goat, don't you?"

"There's a goat?" John said.

"Sure, there's a goat and sheep and didn't Mary McKinney keep a stocked root cellar? Have you looked?"

David gave his wife's shoulder a squeeze. "We'll look. Where are the McGuthries now?"

"They'll be living in London, won't they?"

Sarah felt the panic blossom in her chest. "But the emails I got from her said that there were caretakers. We don't know how to take care of horses, or where to wash our clothes or—"

"Well, sure you'll be needing to take care of the horses. Don't tell me the poor things haven't eaten since you've arrived?"

"They've eaten some grass," John said.

"I suppose there's horse feed in the barn?" David asked.

"There is."

"And the caretakers?" Sarah persisted.

"I'll not be knowing anything about any caretakers. Unless it's yourselves."

"We're the caretakers. Great."

"Who's been taking care of the horses until now?" David asked.

"Likely that would be the Kennedys. They live about five miles t'other side. Now they know you're there, they'll leave it to you, I imagine."

"How much for this lantern?" David pointed to a kerosene lantern sitting high up on a corner shelf.

"Sure, there's bound to be ten of 'em at your place."

"I'd like it all the same," David said, reaching for his wallet. "And I see you still have matches and a jug of kerosene."

As David and the shopkeeper busied themselves filling a small but essential shopping bag, Sarah stepped outside and looked down the deserted village street. John followed her.

"Will we get rickets?"

"What, sweetie?"

"Rickets. We read about it in school. When you don't get fresh fruit and stuff your bones start to go bad."

"No. We'll find fresh fruit and vegetables."

"How about a hamburger?"

"That may be a bit trickier."

A few moments later, David joined them.

"She said she'll hold our lantern and fuel 'til we're ready to leave. There's a little restaurant down the way," he nodded down the street. "Siobhan thinks they're still serving. Guess the locals don't eat out much."

"Siobhan?"

"Yeah, I think she means to be helpful. She's just Irish-y."

"Let's eat, guys," John said, pulling his parents down the street.

Sarah walked ahead of David. Maybe because she didn't look like she was walking *with* anyone, a man coming toward them in the opposite direction got eye contact. He was thin and young and dirty. Her first impulse was to smile, as she might at the drive-through of a fast food restaurant, so it startled her when the man leered at her.

Sarah noted his filthy beard and scruffy clothes which looked like he'd slept in them. She smelled him as he walked past. Stung by his visual assault, she turned to get David's attention as the man passed.

"Did you see that?" she said. But David was looking at the shuttered and dark village windows. He met her eyes with a distracted, vacant look that told her he wasn't listening or even seeing her.

Sarah shook off her annoyance and focused on keeping up with her son.

"Wait for us, John," she called, hurrying to catch up with him and leaving David to his reflections.

LATER THAT AFTERNOON, stuffed with mutton and potatoes, they collected their purchases from Siobhan's store and made the long walk home. John was tired and fretful. Sarah began limping before they had even turned the first corner out of town. And David's shoulders were aching from carrying the heavy bag by the time, four and a half hours later, they finally walked into the frontcourt of their cottage at twilight.

David opened the door to the dark interior of the cottage. He went in first and set the bag down.

"Power is definitely out," he called to them. "Give me a sec to get the lantern lit."

"I'm tired, Mom."

Sarah wrapped her arms around him, grateful they were so far away from the destruction and confusion of what was happening at home, and then feeling instantly anxious for her parents and what they might be experiencing at that very moment. It seemed like such a basic, little thing, she thought, to have a warm, well-lit place in which to curl up tonight.

"I know, angel. Just a few more seconds and you'll be in bed."

A few moments later, the one room of the cottage glowed warmly from the kerosene lantern.

Later that night, as John slept soundly in the big bed, Sarah and David sat on the porch with the lantern between them and finished off a bottle of Pinot Noir.

"I can't imagine what's happening at home," Sarah said, shivering in her heavy sweater.

"I know."

"And you don't have any theories about what happened? That's so unlike you."

David sighed. "From what I saw," he said, speaking deliberately as if carefully choosing every word, "and from what Siobhan heard from other people in the area, I think what happened is that a nuclear bomb exploded over London or maybe the Irish Sea."

"Oh, my dear God."

"And the reason that's my best guess," he said, putting his arm around Sarah and giving her a reassuring squeeze, "is because of the big flash we saw earlier and because none of our electronics work any more."

"Nuclear radiation did this?"

"No, it's called electromagnetic pulse. It's hard to explain but the results of it are pretty much what we're experiencing now."

"If it *is* this electromagnetic thing, how long until things get back to normal?"

"That's just it. Everything has to be rebuilt. All the cellphone towers are fried, all the cars, the power grid. It's a total destruction of the infrastructure."

Sarah stared out into the dark Irish night.

"Oh, my God," she said, her voice a whisper.

"I'm sure people are already working on rebuilding things. But it will take time."

"In the meantime, we're safe?"

"We're safe."

She tilted her face up and they kissed and then sat in silence a moment. Sarah could see David was working something out in his mind.

"What are you thinking?" she asked.

"Just wondering," he said, rubbing her arm and looking out into the black Irish night. "Where do you imagine that damn goat is?"

WHEN THEY AWOKE the next morning, Sarah made cheese sandwiches and mugs of tea for breakfast. The first thing they did was locate the root cellar. They found potatoes, two cases of a decent Côte de Rhône, three bags of flour, sweet feed for the horses, and several dozen tins of meat.

David dragged a bag of feed out and the three of them went into the stables. It was obvious that the horses' stalls had not been mucked for weeks.

"Oh, shit," Sarah said.

"Yeah. Literally," David said.

"What do we do?" John asked, holding his nose.

"First, we get them out of here to someplace where they won't run away so we can feed them and clean out their stalls," Sarah said. "I'll do one and you do one," she said to David. "And *you* stay out of the way so you don't get kicked," she said to John.

"Aw, Mom."

Sarah took a leather halter off the hook in front of the first stall.

"I can't believe we're on our own with these animals. Unbelievable."

She opened the stall door. The name "Dan" was on a tarnished metal plaque on the door.

"Whoa, there, Dan," she said as she stepped into the stall. "Just gonna arrange breakfast and do a linen change, big guy." Carefully, she approached the horse and slipped the halter over his head. "Hand me the lead, will you, David?"

He looked around.

"It's like a big rope or leash," she said, buckling the halter. The horse was big, at least seventeen hands. He was a dark bay with a blaze on his forehead. Sarah was grateful for his calmness and tried to force herself to relax.

David handed her the leather lead he found hanging on the wall. She clipped it to the halter and led the horse out of the stall.

"We'll put them all in the paddock while we clean up. God, what a mess. My shoes are already ruined."

She stood, frozen for a moment, staring at the manure and holding the rope attached to the horse.

"What are we going to do, David?"

"I thought you said we needed to get them out first," David said.

"No, I mean about everything." Sarah looked over her shoulder to make sure John was still outside tossing the ball he had found against the wall of the house. "Don't you think we should try to get to Limerick? There should be an American consulate there."

"Sarah, no." David shook his head. "If this *was* some kind of nuclear bomb that went off then there could be a risk of nuclear contamination in the cities."

"I just don't think staying here is a good idea." She looked around for a place to tie up the horse. She knew she was telegraphing her anxiety and frustration to the animal. He had started to stamp his feet and that made her more nervous. "We can't even feed ourselves here. I want us to go to Limerick."

"Okay, Sarah, that's crazy. How are we going to get there? Walk? It's like two hundred miles or something."

"You just made that up!"

"It doesn't matter how far away it is." He jabbed a pitchfork into a pile of manure and narrowly missing his shoe. "Even if the cities aren't radioactive, it's still a bad idea. For one thing, Americans aren't going to be too popular wherever we go."

"What do you mean?"

"I mean whatever happened, it's because of *us*. You get that, right? Either someone did this to us and the UK is paying the price of being our friend, or we retaliated. But *however* it went down it still adds up to the Americans being the ones at the center of this disaster."

Sarah stared at him, the will to fight left her as the realization of what he was saying began to sink in.

"Should we...should we stay away from town, do you think? There are no laws now to protect us." She clasped her hands as the fear sifted through her. "Should we stay away from Balinagh even?"

"I don't know," David said, picking up the pitchfork again. "But I do think we're safer here in the country on a whole bunch of different levels."

"Mom, I saw rubber boots in the room where all the saddles are hanging."

Sarah hadn't noticed John enter the barn and wondered how much he had heard.

"Oh, thanks, sweetie." She gave David a *this-isn't-over* look and untied the horse, Dan, to lead him out to the paddock.

"See if there are a pair for me, too," he called after her.

AN HOUR LATER, all the horses had been fed and their stalls cleaned. David threw the pitchfork onto the muck cart and pulled the cart behind the barn where there was a huge pile of manure.

"I wonder if I have a job to go home to," he said as he dumped the steaming horse manure onto the pile.

"I guess we won't know until communications have been restored." Sarah came up behind him, and wiped her hands on a towel.

He looked up at her. "That might take months."

"And you think we should just live *here* in the meantime?"

"Got any better ideas?"

She looked at the pile of horse manure. "My God, how our lives have changed in the blink of an eye."

"Come on," he said, grabbing the cart to steer it back around the barn. "Let's find the damn goat."

The goat was in the pasture with a kid.

John was delighted. "Isn't he cute, Mom?" He laughed as the baby goat jumped around him.

"Does this mean we can't milk her?" Sarah asked.

"Were you going to milk her?" David asked with surprise.

"Well, I assume that's what Siobhan meant when we said we needed milk and she referenced the goat."

David laughed. "God, this keeps getting weirder and weirder."

"Do we let them run wild out here?" Sarah looked at the huge pasture. "I mean, is this where they live?"

"Beats the heck out of me."

"Do we feed them? You can't make very nice milk if we don't feed them grain, do you think?"

"Sarah, I have no idea. I'm a city boy."

"Lotta help that is!" she said, laughing. "Just what I need on a farm in rural Ireland in the middle of a damn blackout with no food and no clue—an accountant."

He grinned. "Well, I suppose I could do a full cost-benefit analysis."

"Yeah, that'd be helpful. God knows, you'll have time to do it, too."

They both laughed.

"Are you guys okay?" John asked, frowning. He was holding the squirming kid in his arms.

"We're losing it!" Sarah said, still laughing.

"Well, I wish you'd both chill," he said. "You've got a child to think of." Which just set them off even more, with David holding his sides and tears coursing down his face.

That night they ate salted baked potatoes without butter and canned meat from the root cellar that looked and tasted like shredded Spam. John revisited his rickets question.

"Look," Sarah said. "It's only September so there should be berry patches somewhere. Tomorrow we'll go looking. And there's a jar of jam in the cabinet—"

"With nothing to put it on," John complained.

"I'm going to make bread tomorrow."

"You are?" David asked.

"We've got salt and water and bags of flour in the cellar. I don't think I even need yeast."

"Eggs would be good," David said as he got up to clear the table. "I wonder if we can meet up with our neighbors and maybe trade something for some eggs."

"How would we cook 'em? We'll need butter or lard. This is all so difficult."

"Let's just take it one step at a time."

"Who knows we're here?" John asked.

"What do you mean? Our whole family knows we're in Ireland."

"But what if they've all been killed?"

"Don't even say that, John. Our family is fine, I know it. They're probably working right this minute to try to get us home."

"What if it's worse for them? Maybe they don't even have a house? At least we have a roof."

The rain began again as if to underscore the point.

"Trust me, sweetie," Sarah said as she kissed him. "If no one comes for us, we'll get back home on our own somehow."

"Promise?"

"Absolutely." She looked at David and he nodded.

"Promise, son," he said.

SOMETIME IN THE middle of the night, Sarah put a hand out to touch her husband's shoulder but felt only the cold place where his body had been in the bed. She saw his silhouette as he stood at the living room window. She watched him staring out into the dark night. She knew there was nothing to see.

Watching him, she could feel the anxiety and tension pinging off him in waves. "David?" she whispered.

He turned but made no move toward the bed. "Go back to sleep, Sarah," he said. "I'll be there in a bit." His voice sounded hoarse and muffled—as if he'd been crying.

Sarah lay back down but now she couldn't sleep either.

4

The first week of the crisis brought relentless worry, boredom, insecurity and joy into their daily lives. Unlike their hurried mornings back in the States, the days now began slowly. Sarah woke to the feel of her husband and son nestled beside her. Her husband was wiry and angular, solid and secure against the uncertainty of the coming day. Her son was soft and tender, dreaming his little-boy dreams. She kissed David on his unshaven cheek.

The morning light peeked in between the gaps in the curtains. It was cold outside and the floor of the small cottage was like ice to bare toes. Sarah took a long breath and relished the feeling of her family safe in her arms. This was the time each morning when worry about her parents crept into her thoughts. She had gotten more adept at pushing the thoughts aside realizing that they didn't make her any more capable for the challenges of a coming day.

"I'll make tea," her husband murmured into his pillow. He got out of bed and threw several logs in the woodstove.

"What's on the agenda for today?" he asked.

Sarah snuggled down into the covers. "Well, we were supposed to take a bike tour along the beach today."

"Really?"

"I don't suppose that's still on."

David stretched. "Very funny."

He filled the teakettle and put it on the woodstove. Then he went outside to get the last of the milk on the porch where they'd placed it to keep it cold.

"I wish we knew what was going on at home," Sarah said.

"Let's go into town and see if there's news," David said.

"Are we gonna ride the horses today?" John said through a yawn as he sat up in bed.

"Hey, guy, how long have you been awake?"

"Don't worry," John said, pulling on his jeans. "You guys didn't say anything important."

"We're going back to Balinagh today," Sarah said.

"I'm not walking," John said flatly.

"We could all use the exercise."

"I want the little brown one," John said to his Dad. "You know? The one with the white blob between his eyes?"

"That's called a star," his mother said.

"So I'll call him Star," John said happily. "Which one do you want, Dad?"

David poured tea into three mugs. "Maybe we should take some time getting familiar with our mode of transportation first," he said.

"Maybe there's a horse cart!" John looked from parent to parent with growing excitement. "I'll look in the barn."

"Let's approach one challenge at a time," Sarah said, but she couldn't help but think: *Would the bike tour have been as much fun for John?*

"Right," David said, settling on the bed with them. "We'll have our tea and rustle up some kind of breakfast, then go check to see how to work the horses."

. . .

THIRTY MINUTES later Sarah looked at David with worry and misgiving. They stood in the middle of the small paddock. The two horses and one pony were tacked up and stood quietly.

"Now, remember, John," Sarah said. "This is not like a go-cart—"

"Mom, I know." He reached for the reins to the pony. "I've ridden before."

"This is *not* like how you've ridden before, John. This is not nose-to-tail riding. You have to actually control him."

John faced the pony and called over his shoulder: "Somebody give me a boost up."

"Come on, Sarah," David said. He patted the quiet bay gelding that he would ride. "It'll be fine. Up you go, sport." He lifted his son onto the pony and helped him get his feet into the stirrups.

"This helmet is too big for me, Mom. It keeps dropping down in front of my eyes."

"You have to wear a hard hat, John. Just walk around the paddock and get used to it."

"Need a leg up?" David handed Sarah the reins of the big bay named Dan.

"I forgot," she said. "You used to ride a little?"

"Kind of," he said, lacing his fingers to boost her up. "Had a girl friend in high school who rode."

With a sigh, Sarah bent her knee and accepted the lift up onto the large bay's back. She took a deep breath, felt the horse move beneath her, and then exhaled. Her hands collected the reins and her legs tucked around him as if she'd never stopped riding.

Now that she was on, she felt herself relaxing just a bit. She watched John jogging along the fence line. His hat was bobbing up and down on his head.

David swung into the saddle of his horse.

Sarah shifted her weight and closed her calves around Dan. The horse moved toward the center of the ring.

"Wait up, John," she called. "Let me fix your helmet."

He smiled broadly. "This is so great, Mom. Star is really easy to ride. I'm ready to go!"

Sarah smiled, but the pit of fear and uneasiness returned to her stomach at the thought of venturing out of the paddock along the roadway. She adjusted the buckle on his helmet for a tighter fit.

"Try that, sweetheart."

David trotted over to them.

"Everybody ready?" he said. "I figure if it takes us four hours to walk it, it should only take us two by horseback to get there, stay a couple hours and two hours back. We don't want to get back in the dark."

"David, I'm not sure about this. Why don't we take some time to get comfortable with the horses first?" Sarah said. "If they haven't been ridden in awhile, they could easily decide to take off for Balinagh at a dead run." The feeling of panic would not go away. She knew she was transmitting her unease to her horse.

"It's just," David said, "that if we don't go now we'll have to put it off until tomorrow."

"Yes, but if we put it off 'til tomorrow, I'll be more relaxed. And I'll have made sandwiches from the bread I was going to make today."

"It's okay, Dad," John said. "We can just practice ride today."

Sarah realized, although he'd done a good job of hiding the fact, David was anxious to get word on their family back home, and the status of things. She leaned over and squeezed his hand.

"Let's don't rush it, darling," she said. "We can't afford any accidents, okay?"

David nodded. "Of course. No problem. Come on, sport. Let's check out who our neighbors are." They moved through the open paddock gate.

"Which way, do you think?" he said, squinting down the road.

"I guess we should just follow the road," Sarah said, grateful that at least there wouldn't be cars on it.

"I'll lead," John said.

He trotted ahead of them between ancient, moss-covered drystone walls down the narrow, winding drive that led away from the cottage. The horizon was almost treeless. Sarah tried to remember how far away the ocean was. She thought she could smell it. The sun came out from behind wispy grey clouds to warm their backs as they rode.

"Just move with your pony," Sarah called to John.

"Relax, Sarah. He's doing fine. How about you?"

"I just know how easy an accident can happen," she said, as she slid her hand under the girth on Dan to see if it was tight enough.

They trotted down the one-lane country road without seeing another soul.

"How long do you think we'll be stuck here?" Sarah said.

"I don't know," David said. "Maybe a few months. Maybe longer."

"You think we'll be home by Christmas?"

"I have no idea. I hope so." He trotted his horse to catch up to John.

Sarah watched them both on the road ahead of her. Her spine stiffened, which slowed her horse. *Not be home before Christmas? Was that possible?* Her mind raced to remember all the appointments in the next few months back home that would have to be rescheduled, all the bills that would go unpaid. *Would they lose the house? Was the house still there?*

Instead of relaxing, Sarah felt the worry and anguish overcome her. Within minutes, her thoughts turned to the specific, incapacitating anxiety that hovered just beneath the surface of her every waking moment: *what had happened back home? Were her parents still alive?* As her son and husband rode ahead of her, oblivious, Sarah began to sob silently into the one hand that wasn't clutching her horse's mane for dear life.

. . .

MACK FINN SAT in a plastic lawn chair outside the broken down caravan, a small pile of cigarette butts at his feet. His hands rested on his knees as he stared out across the scrubby Irish landscape. *How strange that the world could look so totally different,* he marveled, from one day to the next. Just yesterday, his bastard old uncle had physically thrown him into *that* bush just beyond his favorite pissing spot, and now the old sot was lying there himself, nearly but not quite buried beneath a quarter foot of muck and mud and weeds.

And wasn't it Mack Finn, himself, who put the old tosser there?

He heard the soft sound of crunching gravel just over his left shoulder as someone approached from the rear. He waited.

"Oy, Mack." The young boy stood near the end of the trailer, as if afraid.

Finn lazily beckoned him to approach. He didn't take his eyes off the brown and grey landscape of the Irish autumn. He didn't look at the faltering, approaching boy.

"Dee-Dee says I'm to ask ya what we're to eat," the boy mumbled, rubbing his dirty hands up in down his jeans in a nervous gesture.

Finn could smell the boy's fear and it made him smile. *With Uncle Liam gone,* he thought with satisfaction, *they'll all be afraid of me now.*

The eldest of five children in a poor gypsy family that once numbered in the hundreds, Finn felt the rank of protector and guardian of the flock which had finally, belatedly, come to him. Proud of the fact that he had left school at eleven—*been forced to when he was caught trying to root that daft scanger in the class behind his*—Finn grew up rough and he grew up ready. No one had given him a break. No one had given him a hand. Now, at twenty-two, he'd already spent seven years in an English prison learning more than school could ever teach him.

He leaned back into the chair and listened for the songbirds in the trees surrounding the old trailer. They sounded particularly sweet this morning, he decided. As if they knew that a better new world was coming. A world that was uninterested in rules or laws. A world that belonged to the strong and the fearless. Finn smiled to himself, enjoying the sun on his face and the birdsong.

Life may have come apart at the seams for everyone else. But for Mack Finn, it had just clicked into place.

5

An hour into the ride, Sarah knew the horses were docile and well mannered. Even though David and John had much less riding experience than she did, they both rode as if they had ridden for years.

Sarah was amazed at the ease with which her son rode his pony—no fear, no hesitation in letting the animal know what he wanted. David likewise wasn't being thrown to the ground or run off with. Sarah knew she had psyched herself out with horses many years ago. Now she had living proof that it was all in her head. She watched John turn his pony off the road into the bordering field to explore it.

Her cry had done her good. She was still worried, but the tension in her gut seemed to have eased. When John trotted up beside her she realized she had been holding her breath.

"Isn't this great, Mom?" he asked, his face pink with fresh air. "Isn't Star a great pony? We gotta bring him home with us." He nudged the pony into a trot on the dirt road to ride next to his dad. David pointed to a running rabbit along the rock wall.

Sarah smiled, and she could feel the knot in her stomach diminish. She could also feel Dan loosen up when she smiled.

"Poor Dan," she said. "Your friends got happy-go-lucky green riders and you got the basket case." She leaned down and patted his neck.

David trotted back to her. "I think there's a farm up ahead. If there's anyone home, we can find out about our caretakers."

Sarah squinted in the direction he was indicating. "Maybe *they* are our caretakers."

Within minutes the three of them turned down a long dirt drive that led to a small cottage with a barn, much like their own place. A dog barked and ran to meet them.

"He looks unfriendly," John said.

"He's just alerting his owners," David said. "Aren't you, boy?"

An old man stepped into the courtyard and silenced the dog with a hand signal as they rode up.

"Hello," David said. "We're your neighbors from the McKinney Cottage." He smiled broadly. The man said nothing.

"The Americans?" David continued. "We're renting the cottage?" He turned to Sarah and said, "Maybe he doesn't speak English?"

"Might only speak Irish," she said. She smiled at the man who only narrowed his eyes. His fingers reached down and tightened on his dog's collar.

"I think we're freaking him out, David. Let's leave."

"I thought the Irish were on our side," John said, as they turned their horses and started back towards the main road.

Just then, an old woman came out into the yard. "Hello," she called. "Are you the Americans next door?"

"Yes, that would be us," David said.

"Oh, come in, come in," she said. "You're all very welcome. And this your little lad, is it? What a handsome boy! Come in all of you." She thumped the old man on the arm. "Have you gone totally daft, man? They're the *Americans*. And you just standing there like some kind of *ejeet*."

They steered their horses back to the cottage. The woman

wore a long woolen skirt and looked like she'd stepped out of the last century. She wiped her hands on a dishtowel tucked into her waistband.

"Oh, it's good they're getting some exercise," she said, patting Dan on the neck. "Sure, it's one good bit of luck in all this that you're not useless around horses." She laughed and winked at John. "Come in, please. Seamus will take the horses." She touched the older man on the shoulder and spoke abruptly to him in Gaelic.

Sarah dismounted and handed the reins to Seamus. "I'm Sarah Woodson and this is my husband David and our son John."

The older woman stuck her hand out and they shook.

"I'm Dierdre McClenny and this is Seamus whom I guess you already met."

"I'm so glad to meet you," Sarah said.

"John and I will help Mr. McClenny with the horses," David said as he dismounted.

The woman ushered Sarah into her cottage, a miserable looking hovel from the outside, but surprisingly warm and cozy on the inside. Sarah could smell bread baking.

"Sit, sit," the woman said, motioning to a chair belonging to an old metal dinette set. "I'll just put the kettle on."

Sarah sank into the seat, realizing that her knees were weak but whether from the ride or the situation in general, she couldn't be sure.

"Mrs. McClenny, do you know what happened? I mean, do you have any information?"

"Oh, please call me Dierdre. About the war, you mean?" Dierdre set out three chipped mugs and opened the small refrigerator for a carton of milk. Sarah noticed the interior light was out.

She stuttered. "We're at...it's a war?" She had to steady herself with her hands against the table.

"May as well be, my dear," Dierdre said. "We were afraid you wouldn't be able to get out and about. Most Americans aren't interested in riding. Wouldn't know one end from the other."

"Do you and Seamus get out?" Sarah looked around the room. It was simple but tidy and clean. "Do you have a car?"

"A car?" Dierdre laughed. "Not for ages now. We have a gig, you see." She moved to the stove to get the kettle. She poured the hot water into an old brown teapot on the kitchen counter. "Seamus and I will be fine. In fact, no different, really." She brought the teapot to the table. "We've got eggs, preserved fruit and jam and I always put away what I grow over the summer. We'll be fine, please God."

She poured the tea into two mugs. "What about yourself? Have you been able to get word back to your people in America?"

Sarah shook her head and felt tears welling up. "No way to reach them," she said. She could hear David and John talking outside the cottage. John was laughing.

Dierdre nodded and dropped sugar and milk into Sarah's tea without asking. She handed the mug to Sarah.

"Well, we'll all hear when we're meant to. Meanwhile, there's us getting on and getting by."

The tea was hot and it helped. Sarah felt better after just a few sips.

"I'm not sure how we'll survive out here," Sarah said.

Dierdre frowned. "Surely, you're joking? You have a child. You'll do what you have to."

"Yes, but if you don't know what it is you have to do, how can you do it?" Sarah knew she sounded weak and whiny. She imagined that—if Dierdre knew their lives in Florida—Sarah would look very rich and spoiled compared to her simple Irish country life.

"Well, you'll learn, my dear," the older woman said kindly. "You'll take it one day at a time and you'll learn." She patted Sarah's hand. "And you have neighbors. We'll help each other. You've met the Kennedys?"

Sarah drained her tea mug. "Not yet. We thought you might be them."

Dierdre laughed. "Now you'll not want to be insulting me before we've had a chance to get to know each other." She laughed at her own joke and Sarah laughed too. It felt like years since she had laughed.

"Hey, what's so funny, guys?" David said as he poked his head in the cottage. "I don't want to track mud into your kitchen, Dierdre."

Dierdre stood up and ushered David and John into the house. "Don't be silly, now. The very idea! And with Himself tracking in every manner of dirt all day long. Your tea's right here." She went to fetch another mug.

"Where's Seamus?" Sarah asked David.

"He's with the horses, Mom," John said. "You know, you can't understand a word he says."

Dierdre returned and poured two more mugs of tea.

"He's a bit of an odd duck, is our Seamus," she said, handing David and John their tea mugs. "Sit, sit. Are you heading somewhere today or just visiting the neighbors?"

David sat down next to Sarah.

"Well, we were just exploring, really, any place we can get to and back before dark."

"If I can talk you into staying, we'd be proud to share our supper with you. It's not much, but it's a nice plump chicken so it is and will stretch to five if one of you holds back." She winked at John and he grinned.

Sarah was inclined to say no in order to save the old couple's dinner for them, but the eagerness in John's face combined with her own yearning for company changed her mind.

"If you're sure it's no trouble. That would be great. Thank you."

Dierdre's beaming smile confirmed to Sarah that her reply was the right one.

. . .

"Stop acting the maggot," Finn snarled, ratcheting the rope tighter around the young man's wrist. "We're having a little chat, ya gobshites, so put down your jar." He strutted to the center of the group around a small cook fire and dragged the younger man behind him.

Eight other men sat or stood around the fire smoking and drinking beer. They looked apprehensively at their leader's entrance.

"Anybody see young Billy, here, eat me tea while I was to town?" Finn gave the rope a jerk and could almost feel the poor sod trembling at the other end. The men around the campfire were unshaven and their clothes rags. One seated man had a squirming puppy in his lap. All of them either shook their heads or mumbled negative responses.

Finn knew the boy hadn't eaten his dinner. Billy was a teenager and clearly scared out of his mind. Finn thought Billy might be a cousin although he wasn't sure and didn't care. The little rotter was blubbering now.

"No one saw this gobshite eat me tea?" Finn said, raising his voice. The fear in their faces pleased him.

"I seen 'im, Mack," one man said.

"Okay, Brendon. Thank you. Finally. Someone who tells me the truth." Finn knew it was a lie.

He jerked the rope off the now openly weeping boy and pushed him toward the group. "I can be merciful, Billy," he said loudly, and tossed the rope into the fire. "Remember that. And don't eat me tea no more."

Billy wiped his tearstained face with both hands and nodded.

As Finn turned to leave the group, he stopped abruptly in front of the man with the puppy and scooped the dog up in his arms. Startled, the man jumped to his feet.

"Oy, Mack..." he said, looking nervously at his dog in Finn's arms.

Without looking away, Finn deftly wrung the puppy's neck and tossed it back to the gypsy. "Did you say something, Gerry?"

All the men jumped up.

"Remember, lads," Finn shouted. He was looking at their stunned faces. He grinned and mimicked Brandon's pointing gesture when he had fingered Billy. "I can be *un*forgiving, too."

He put his hand on the shoulder of the man now holding the dead dog. "No money for luxuries, me boyo," Finn said, then turned on his heel and left.

SARAH, David and John left Seamus and Dierdre's in early evening while there was still light left but even so, Sarah could see that John was tired and sagging in his saddle. She watched his pony step knowingly in the deepening shadows of the trail back to the house and she was grateful for the animal's steady temperament.

Dierdre had given them two dozen fresh hen's eggs and two jars of berry jam. David stashed them in his saddlebags as if they were the finest caviar.

The visit had done all of them good. Dierdre told Sarah where to find items in the cottage she didn't even know she needed, and she reminded her to make sure the goats were locked in at night to protect them from roving dog packs. David promised to come back in a few days and help Seamus mend a fence around the hen house.

The hospitality had given Sarah a warm feeling of connection that salved her feeling of isolation and homesickness. It surprised her that someone she had nothing in common with could make her feel so connected.

She was too tired tonight to figure out how that could be but was grateful for her new friend. Her exhaustion and her pleasure at the evening, combined with a full stomach, made the ride a peaceful one without anxiety.

The small bottle of brandy that Dierdre had brought out at the end of the meal had gone a long way to soothing Sarah's jangled nerves about the horses. She was now taking pleasure in the ride, enjoying the feel of the evening air on her skin and the sight of the dear nodding head of the boy who rode beside her. She and David spoke little on the ride home. They were both enjoying their own thoughts as they processed the day's events.

When they got to the house, David pulled John out of the saddle. John stood sleepily beside Sarah while David took the pony's reins.

"Wait here while I put these two to bed then I'll come back for big Dan there," David said.

"Are you sure?" As pleasant as the ride had been, Sarah was tired enough to be very grateful to have David unsaddle the horses. David walked the two horses to the barn, and she stood with her horse and John at the front steps.

Suddenly, she froze. John, sensing the change in her, shook his sleepiness away.

"What is it?" he whispered.

Sarah pulled him away from the front steps.

"The front door's open," she said.

6

They had taken the electronics, the new lanterns and all the food in the cupboards. The lock on the front door was broken and the interior of the cottage was trashed. After minimizing the robbery as much as she could to John, Sarah put him to bed. Then she and David sat on the porch sharing a bottle of wine the thieves had not found.

"We were lucky," David said. "They took mostly the useless stuff."

"Our cell phones? Our television? The iPad?"

"That's right, Sarah. And they left the Gor-Tex jackets. And the axe and the knives."

"I hope they choke on the food."

"They were probably hungry if that's any consolation."

"The food they took was food stolen out of your son's mouth, David."

"Maybe they have a son to feed, too."

"Okay, fine. Whatever. It's not a good thing, though, you know? We're not safe here."

"They waited 'til we left..."

"And what about next time when they don't wait for us to leave first? This...this crisis is not going to bring out the best in people, David." Sarah finished her wine and looked out across the pasture. There was no moon and the fields were black.

"At least they didn't find the wine," David said with a smile.

Sarah sighed. She was glad David could shake it off but for her the pleasure of the day was long gone.

THE NEXT MORNING, David was up early hammering on the house's exterior. Sarah turned her attention to the kitchen and the task of making bread. Dierdre had given her a small yeast starter and while sour dough bread had been her least favorite kind back in the States, she was looking forward to eating it from now on if she could actually produce a loaf.

John came in the front door. "Mom, Dad says the goats have to live with the horses from now on. Is there anything to eat? I'm starving."

"You just ate breakfast." Sarah felt a kernel of anxiety in the pit of her stomach. It was so easy to take care of him back home. She could just pop a toaster streudel in the oven and pour a glass of milk from the fridge. Now, making sure he didn't go hungry was an exhausting and often impossible proposition.

"I'm making bread," Sarah said as she picked up the jar of starter.

"When will that be ready?"

"Not for awhile," she admitted. "Here." She pulled out one of the jars of jam they had gotten from Dierdre. "Eat a spoonful of this."

"Without bread?"

"If you wait a minute, I'll make you a fried egg."

That seemed to satisfy him so she lit the gas stove and put two of the precious eggs in an iron skillet.

John watched her. "You're doing it without butter?"

"I didn't know you knew so much about cooking. I'm going to watch it carefully. It'll be fine." She was not at all sure about that but she didn't have a choice. They had no butter.

David came into the kitchen and dropped a hammer onto the dining table.

"How's that trap coming, son?"

Sarah frowned. "Trap?"

"Oh, yeah," John said. "I'm making a rabbit trap."

"To catch as in for eating?" Sarah tried to keep the note of incredulity out of her voice.

"Well, not for pets, eh, sport?" David laughed. "Lunch?" he said, hopefully to Sarah.

"You just had breakfast."

"Of a sort. Two spoons of jam and tea without sugar or milk. Pretty crappy breakfast."

Sarah added two more eggs to the skillet and felt her own stomach growl. Feeling like she was throwing gemstones down a well, she added a third egg for herself. "We only have seven eggs left. We need to be mindful of our rations."

"I'm going back to Dierdre's tomorrow," David said. "I'll trade my services for another dozen eggs."

"And maybe some milk, Dad?" John took his plate of eggs and sat down at the kitchen table. "I hate drinking tea without milk."

"He needs milk, David," Sarah said, feeling the panic bubbling up in her. "He's a growing boy."

"I'll bring back milk and eggs," David promised. "Don't worry."

They ate quickly and David and John returned to finding ways to safeguard the house and barn while Sarah turned her attention back to the bread-making. Although never much of a baker she had, in one of her more industrious moods, typed in a recipe for bread on her phone. Unfortunately, the robbers had taken all their phones last night. And they didn't work anyway.

Sighing, she tried to remember the ingredient amounts.

Baking is a science, she knew. You could wing it to a certain extent when you cooked, but baking needed exactness. She pulled open drawers in the kitchen, looking for a cookbook.

She glanced at the starter on the counter and knew she couldn't waste it by experimenting. She thought of the disappointment on John's face if she had to tell him tonight there was no bread.

By God, I'm going to make him bread today! Was it so much to ask that I give my child a slice of damn bread?

Sarah crossed the living room and began pulling books off the shelves. They were mostly paperbacks left by previous vacationers. She stacked them carefully—in case they ended up being the only things they had to read for the next few months.

Before she had abandoned paper books entirely and gone strictly to an e-reader, Sarah used to keep her favorite recipes on index cards which she laminated and used for bookmarks. She paused for a moment remembering that. She *did* used to do that. It seemed like decades ago.

She found what she was looking for on the very bottom shelf of the bookcase. And when she did, she literally whooped with delight. Not just a recipe, but a cookbook. And not just any cookbook but *Joy of Cooking*—a cookbook from her very own kitchen, and one she knew as well as a beloved novel. Finding it felt like the first real stroke of luck since the Crisis. Like a turning point, somehow.

AN HOUR LATER, with the dough rising under a thin, worn dishtowel she had found in a kitchen drawer, Sarah walked outside into the sunshine. She felt like she had accomplished something no less significant than whatever David had been doing to shore up their physical defenses.

As the mother, she felt she'd done her job to tend her nest

and protect her hatchling. She was surprised by a stack of wood outside the kitchen door. John had collected and stacked the wood without being told. She scanned the vacant courtyard between the barn and the house.

Maybe, she thought, *just maybe there's some good to all this mess.*

David came out of the barn, wiping his hands on his jeans.

That's not good, Sarah thought. *We don't have an automatic washing machine any more. Unless you count me.*

"Hey," he said, walking toward her, smiling. "I think I've done as much as can be done to secure the place. They'll have to take crowbars to get in next time."

"Great. Horses okay?"

He looked over his shoulder toward the pasture.

"I turned them out," he said. "They were getting skitterish in the paddock."

Just the thought of the horses "skitterish" made Sarah's stomach clench.

"Do you know for a fact that the pasture is fenced?"

He looked at her in surprise. "I thought all pastures were fenced."

"Maybe we'd better do a perimeter check, just to be sure. Where's John?"

"I thought he was in the house."

Sarah literally vibrated with the anxiety that pulsed through her at his words. For a moment, she felt like she might hyperventilate. Instead, she found herself turning toward the pasture at a run.

"Grab the halters," she said. "And catch up with me."

THEY WALKED and called for forty minutes before Sarah turned back. They found all three horses but not John. She led Dan and the pony. David led the big bay he called "Rocky." Both Rocky and the pony had nameplates on their stalls but unlike Dan's theirs were in Gaelic. After a day of struggling to pronounce their names, David and John rechristened the two "Rocky" and "Star."

There was no fence.

"This isn't Mandarin," she said to David, referring to the neighborhood in Jacksonville where they lived. "You can't just let him go do his own thing. He's only ten years old."

"I thought he was with you," David said. "I'm sorry..."

"We were broken into last night! What if those people are still around? What if they have him?"

"Look, Sarah, I know—"

"No, you don't know! You *don't* know, David!"

It took every ounce of emotional strength she had not to verbally launch into David. Some part of her knew he wasn't to blame for John being missing. She had never felt so powerless, so ineffectual, in her whole life, *especially* now when the stakes were so high. She was so upset she didn't even think about the fact that she was leading a horse on either side of her. Her focus was on solely getting her boy back.

"You keep looking for him out here," she said. "I'm going to go see if he's back at the cottage."

"We'll find him, Sarah," David called after her, the fear in his voice belying his words. "I'm sure he's just exploring."

Sarah didn't bother replying. She was angry and afraid, a combination of which she had felt pretty much nonstop since the Crisis had happened. She felt as if her whole world was hanging by a thread, with nothing certain, nothing secure.

It was early afternoon but already it seemed as if the sun had disappeared. The light was grey, the dark clouds scudded across the sky.

What if he gets caught out here and it storms?

One of the horses shied at something in the grass and Sarah dropped the lead rope. She quickly snatched it back and tried to calm him, convinced it was her own anxiety that had caused him to shy in the first place.

Damn horses, she thought. *They can read your mind.*

She took a deep breath and tried to steady her nerves, for their sakes if not her own. She estimated that she was about fifteen minutes from the cottage. If David found John in the pasture and they rode double on Rocky, they would actually beat her back to the house. The thought comforted her and she walked on, pushing thoughts of crumpled little boy forms and wild dogs from her mind.

Cresting the last hill, she saw their cottage below. The courtyard was empty but something caught her eye in the pasture behind the house. A small herd of fluffy white sheep were moving steadily toward the cottage. Sarah looked closer and could see John's red shirt in front of the flock. He was leading the lead sheep with a rope.

Tears of relief came to her eyes. *He was safe.*

He waved and she started down the hill to meet him.

"Where's Rocky?" he asked when they met up.

"Dad's got him. He's up in the far pasture looking for you."

"How come?"

Sarah shifted both lead ropes to one hand and hugged John.

"John," she whispered into his hair. "You scared us to death. We didn't know where you were. Did you tell anyone you were leaving?"

John moved out of her hug. "Mom, stop it. You're pinching me. I didn't realize I *was* leaving until I got the idea about the sheep."

"You must never do that again," Sarah said, gently shaking his shoulder with her free hand.

"Sorry, Mom."

"All right." She steadied herself with a long breath. The fear and anxiety of the last hour would take awhile to abate. "So, what's with the sheep?"

"They're ours." He twisted around to show her the tag in the one sheep's ear that he was leading. "See? It matches the brand at our cottage. You know? The one in the barn on the stalls?"

"Sheep," she said. "That's nice."

"Mom," he said with exasperation. "We can make wool from their fur, you know?"

"Well, let's get them into the paddock. Why were they wandering around out there anyway? Is that where they live?"

"I don't know. But I just thought we should get all the stuff that's ours in one spot, you know?"

"Good logic. Next time *tell* someone you're leaving, though. We were worried."

"Okay," he said, leading the sheep down the hill to the paddock. Sarah let the flock go ahead and followed with the two horses.

LATER THAT NIGHT, after a dinner of perfectly baked bread and scrambled eggs, Sarah sat on the couch with the cookbook on her knees reading about how to make butter from goat's milk. David and John played cards by the fireplace.

"You know, son, we can eat the sheep, too," David said.

"These sheep are not for eating," John said, firmly. "They're for the fur."

"The wool," Sarah said.

"That's right. For sweaters and blankets and stuff. Mom knows how to knit."

All of a sudden the room reverberated with the sound of a shrill scream. David and John were on their feet in an instant.

Sarah shouted: "John, no! Stay here!"

David put his hand on John. He picked up the heavy axe leaning against the fireplace and stepped to the front door. John moved to join him but Sarah grabbed his arm.

"Stay here," she said, the fear throbbing through her with every word.

David jerked open the door and strode out onto the porch.

"Who's there?" he said. Sarah could tell he was making his voice sound deep and threatening. He hesitated and then moved off the porch into the night.

7

They had caught a rabbit.

The loud snap of the trap and the rabbit's scream had heralded the moment when regular fresh meat came back into their lives. The next morning, Sarah noticed that John was very quiet at breakfast. He had successfully held back the tears last night when David brought the still-warm carcass into the kitchen, but had blurted out this morning that he was becoming a vegan.

Sarah fried up the last of the eggs. His tea was black but sweet. They'd found a decent store of sugar in the cellar.

"You know," she said, "God made that rabbit for us," she said. "He put it here to help sustain us."

"To eat, you mean." John pushed his eggs around with his fork and did not look up.

"Yes, to eat..."

"And if that's true, then why did He make them so cute, huh? Answer me that." He shoved his plate away.

"That is a good question with an unknowable answer," Sarah said, trying not to smile.

"You *assume* God made the rabbit for us to eat because that's what you want to do to it. That's what you call..." He looked out the window as if looking for the word out there.

David walked into the kitchen. "It's called *rationalization*," he said.

John stared down at his hands. "Why would He make 'em so cute if He wanted us to kill 'em?" he repeated.

David sat down next to him. "I don't know, son. And I know it's hard because you've always looked at rabbits as pets, but your trap has provided for us, do you see that?" He looked at Sarah and she nodded. "We need the meat and you helped give us that."

John looked up at him. "I provided for the family."

"That's right, son."

John pulled his plate back and picked up his fork.

David looked at Sarah.

"No more eggs left, sorry," she said. "And there is also the little matter of inning-skay the abbit-ray." She made a face and indicated the door that led to the root cellar where they'd put the rabbit.

"Gimme a break. I know *pig*-latin, guys."

David sighed and reached for a slice of cold toasted bread. He spread a scoop of Dierdre's jam on it while Sarah poured him a cup of tepid tea.

"Helluva way to start your day," he said which caused all three of them to start laughing.

IN THE BEGINNING of their second week in Ireland, they learned to milk the goat, and they all developed new habits for securing the house and checking in with each other. David learned how to gut and skin a rabbit (without gagging). Sarah learned to make a delicious rabbit stew using whatever vegetables she found in the root cellar.

· · ·

JOHN LEARNED to gather wood and peat for the fire, to daily reset his rabbit traps, to clean out the horses' stalls with his dad, and to move the sheep from one pasture to another and then home every night to the safety of their paddock. At night, he would clean the horse's leather tack while his dad sharpened their tools and Sarah read to them from one of the paperback mysteries. She made it "family friendly" when needed as she read.

They abandoned plans to ride into town after Dierdre told them she heard that someone had burned an American flag in one village. Sarah decided it was just as well. It was too far away and they had fallen into a comfortable rhythm with David riding to Seamus and Dierdre's a couple times a week to work for them. The first time, he brought more fresh eggs back with him. The second time, John accompanied him and they brought back a live chicken. David also delivered scribbled instructions from Dierdre on how to weave and comb wool without a loom.

Besides, Sarah thought, *all of this was temporary. Best to just sit tight and ride it out.*

ONE EVENING, after they had been in Ireland a month and it was cold even in the middle of the day, they moved to their usual places in front of the fireplace after dinner. Sarah finished cleaning the dishes and joined the other two who were talking seriously, their respective handiwork of tack and tools ignored. She pulled out the novel she had been reading to them.

"It's 'cause the sheep trust us," John was saying. "I mean, I know Seamus says it's 'cause they're stupid— "

"You got Seamus to talk?" Sarah said as she sat down.

"But they're not stupid," he said. "They just know that we know what's best for them."

David poked a log in the fireplace. "They all know that?" he asked, smiling.

"Well, no," John admitted. "Sometimes one here or there gets his own ideas about stuff, but it almost always ends badly, you know? Like when the big shaggy one, you know, Orca? With the gimpy leg? Got stuck in the ditch over by Blue Rock?"

Sarah said, "How do you know the name of the rock?"

John gave her a barely tolerant look. "I don't know the real name of it. It's big and blue so that's what I call it. Anyway, he was trying to get to that old deer salt lick and got trapped in the ditch because he didn't think things through, you know?"

David stared at his son. "How old are you again?"

John dumped the bridle he was working on to the floor next to him.

"Okay, Mom, she's about to be murdered in the basement, right?" He looked at his dad. "Why do girls always go down to the basement when they hear a noise? Are they just stupid or what?"

Sarah cleared her throat, gave her son a baleful look, and began to read.

THE NEXT MORNING, after their chores, they got a surprise when they looked up to see Seamus and Dierdre coming down the long drive in their pony and trap. They came bearing two chickens and a rooster, another dozen eggs, a kidney and potato pie, and a newspaper. The newspaper was printed in Draenago, one town over from Balinagh, and there was no knowing how factual the information was.

The old couple had been to Balinagh the day before. David and John helped Seamus unhitch the pony and put it in the paddock with a flake of hay while Sarah made a pot of tea in the kitchen. She had tried her hand at a basic loaf cake the day before, no icing, but was as proud to serve it up to Dierdre with their tea as if it had been a Lindser Torte.

The older woman seemed tired to Sarah. But likely it was the additional news she brought that contributed to the lines of worry on her face.

"We heard of a friend of a friend, from the village," Dierdre said, after Sarah poured her a second cup of tea. "The villains broke into his house, murdered poor Iain, and ransacked his croft."

Sarah was horrified. Her eyes flickered through the kitchen window to the sounds of her son's laughter as he talked with Seamus and David.

"Murdered?" she said as she sat down heavily in a kitchen chair.

"Aye," Dierdre said. "Took everything, so they did, and left the animals to wander. That's how they discovered the murder. One of his cows was found dead, too far from Iain's place, and someone went to check on Iain."

"Are you worried about the two of you?" Sarah asked.

"Sure I am. Me an old woman and an addle-pated old man? We're sitting ducks, so we are." It unnerved Sarah to see how upset Dierdre was. Up until today she'd always been so steady and self-assured.

"Do you...I mean, is there any way to protect yourselves?" Sarah asked.

"Guns, you mean? Oh, aye, but Iain had guns too. A fat lot of good they did him, lying in his own gore."

"Did he have dogs?"

"Shot dead, both of them, and never raised a whimper to warn him."

"Do you think the killers were someone who knew the dogs? I mean it would explain why they didn't bark."

"Aye, it would," Dierdre said, as if realizing for the first time something very important. "They didn't bark because they knew them. Iain was killed by someone he knew." She looked at Sarah and, if anything, the fear seemed to be more intense than before.

Later, when the couple took their leave, David went with them for the night. After seeing how upset Dierdre was, Sarah encouraged him to.

"We'll be fine," she said, her stomach jumping with anxiety. "Get them settled in and reassured the best you can. It's just one night."

That night, Sarah and John sat in front of the fireplace as usual.

"Feels weird, Dad not being here," John said.

"I know."

"Are you okay, Mom? You look nervous."

Sarah saw that John looked nervous too. Afraid his insecurity might be the result of her nerves, she smiled and shook her head.

"Not at all. Just missing Dad's company. We're really the Three Musketeers, aren't we? Just feels wrong not to all be here, that's all."

"Yeah, I know what you mean."

"Ready to hear chapter eight then?" she asked, picking up the book.

"Yeah, sure. Hey, you know, Mom?"

"Yes, sweetie?"

"If it'd make you feel better, you can always keep the gun loaded while Dad's away."

FIFTEEN MINUTES later Sarah sat at the kitchen table staring at the small rifle.

"Dad said not to tell you," John said. "He said you'd freak out about a gun in the house."

Sarah ran a hand through her hair.

"Where did it come from?" she asked. It looked lethal just sitting there, as if it could harm the two of them without even being touched.

"Dad found it in the barn."

"Does it have bullets?"

John opened a kitchen drawer and withdrew a small cardboard box which he pushed across the table to her.

"Does Dad know how to shoot it?" she asked.

"He said he had a rifle when he was a kid."

Sarah looked at her son as if there were more to the story.

John shrugged and nodded to the gun.

"How hard can it be?" he said.

Sarah lifted the rifle gingerly. It was very heavy.

"It's not loaded," John said.

"Okay," Sarah said, putting the gun back down and taking a long breath. "Do we know how to load it?"

Her son grinned at her.

8

_____

The next morning, they woke up to frost on the ground. With no central heat, Sarah and John moved about the cottage in their Gor-Tex jackets over sweaters like tubby Michelin men. John's jacket was so big, he had to fold the sleeves back. He wanted to cut them but Sarah wouldn't allow it.

What if we're here long enough for him to grow into them?

John lit the fire in the cook stove and gathered more wood, set the rabbit traps, fed the horses and the goats and the chickens, and sharpened the knives.

Sarah watched in amazement. *I wouldn't even let him open a can of dog food back home for fear he'd cut himself,* she thought.

While he did his chores, Sarah put water on for tea, sliced bread and put it on the stovetop to toast, then scrambled six eggs in the iron skillet. Dierdre had shown her how to make butter from the goat's milk and she was going to try that today. They were all, finally, at the point where they didn't mind the taste of the goat's milk in their tea.

She needed more soap—for the dishes, for their clothes, for their baths. She intended to heat up water today so John could have a nice long soak in the tub. She couldn't remember the last time the child had been clean. Probably at the hotel in Limerick.

Later, she helped John bring the sheep in from the pasture and the horses from the paddock. She found herself looking up repeatedly to see if David might appear on the horizon. She expected him any time.

The weather was biting cold and the wind had picked up. Even so, before dinner—a cold dinner of leftover rabbit with green tomato preserves from the larder—she set John to constructing a target of straw in the back pasture. She fetched the rifle from the kitchen and the box of rounds. With shaking fingers, she fumbled a round into the side port. She held the gun muzzle away from her as if frozen.

"You gotta cock it," John said.

She looked at him, frowning.

"Slide that part up and it drops in." He pointed to the cocking mechanism.

"Dear God in Heaven, how do you know that?" She shook her head, slid the action forward and heard the sounds of the bullets dropping into the chamber.

"I saw it on YouTube."

"Remind me to watch you closer." She held out another round.

"You can't put that in port side," John said. "It has to go underneath."

Sarah took another breath and scanned the horizon for strength and perspective and then did something that she never in a million years would have imagined herself doing. She handed the gun to her son.

"Show me."

The boy took the rifle. He turned facing the scarecrow and pointed the gun in that direction.

"The guy on the YouTube video said the best way to load a gun is not to take your eyes off your tactical environment...that's the thing you're aiming at." Without looking away from the scarecrow, he palmed the clip horizontally in his right hand and, following the trigger guide forward, shoved it into the magazine from underneath.

"Okay," Sarah said, trying to remember that her grandfather and his whole generation had been familiar with firearms since they were children. "Just two shots apiece to save ammunition, okay?" she said.

John's first shot went straight to the straw man's head. But the recoil knocked him flat. He backed up twenty yards and planted his left foot forward, the heel of his right behind the left. He took careful aim at the target. His second shot also went to the head and this time he stayed on his feet.

Sarah's first shot hit the body and the second one missed entirely. *At least I didn't fall down,* she thought grimly, but the anticipation of the recoil made her even more fearful of the gun.

After that, they practiced loading the gun until they could both do it quickly and without looking.

That night, David came home exhausted with a bandaged hand, bringing soap and a bag of flour. Sarah watched him ride up over the knoll and realized, for the first time, that the sight of him felt like an answer to prayer. He waved off dinner, saying Dierdre had practically stuffed him before he left their place. He opted instead for a quick wash up with soap before collapsing by the fire with John, who gave him a blow-by-blow account of all his chores and the various antics of their animals.

Sarah read a short note from Dierdre, full of apologies for "being such a ninny" the day before. It made her realize that just because she couldn't mail a letter to her folks didn't mean she couldn't write one. She had found a large supply of loose leaf paper and several ball point pens in the kitchen drawer. Just the thought of talking to her parents—even if it was one-sided—made her feel closer to them.

After a paragraph of what could only be considered serious

whining, Sarah crumpled up the letter and started over. She told her parents that they were fine. That's not a lie, she thought with surprise. She said she prayed they were, too.

So, how to describe our daily round here? We live in a one-room cottage, with the nearest market really more of a convenience store and it nearly ten miles away. It's been a little over three weeks since we got here and now people only gather at the store to trade and swap news. I don't know how it is there, but the news here changes from day to day and most of it sounds made up so we don't put too much stock in it.

There haven't been any goods for sale at the store since a couple days after the crisis, but people have lots of stuff to trade: fish, produce, horses, milk, homemade beer (don't ask). There is only one road leading to our cottage and that's made of dirt and rock. It's okay for horses, bad for cars. (Which, of course, works out okay these days.) There's no cars!

The people who own our cottage left a storage cellar of food, mostly for the horses. There's a pot-bellied stove that keeps the cottage warm at night, a fireplace that we rarely use because we lose too much heat, *and a cook stove that we use all the time. There is, of course, no electricity so there's no TV, no radio, and no water heater, so we have to boil water on the stove (meaning we have to gather wood first) if we want a warm bath or to wash the dishes properly. There's an ancient washer that's really just a mechanical hand-crank thing that works because it's powered by me but no dryer.*

The nights are still and you can see every star in the firmament one by one. The mornings are crystal blue and so bright at first that it hurts your eyes. Our days are very busy. (You probably guessed that since we have to find firewood before we can make a fire before we can heat the water before we can wash the breakfast dishes! Ha ha!)

After the effort of producing a meal of some kind and then cleaning up afterwards, you have to feed the animals and not get stepped on, cut, pinched or bruised in the process. In the middle of all that, there is an incredible silence and stillness—in your mind, in your ears, in your thoughts. Sometimes the world is so quiet here I think it must be like what it was for our ancestors a hundred years earlier.

After all that hard work, you read if it's still light enough, you take long walks–to check on the animals usually—that freeze your feet and your ears and burn your cheeks. And then when you return to the cottage, you try to get warm again, or dry if it's rained on your walk which it almost always does, or find something to eat that won't cause terrible gas or constipation the next day. No wonder the Irish drink!

SARAH LOOKED over the letter and felt a little better. Reading it seemed to help put it in perspective. She noticed that David had fallen asleep in his chair and John was working out a move on the chessboard by the fireplace. Every once in awhile he got up and added a stick to the fire. She folded the letter and tucked it inside the *Joy of Cooking* cookbook.

"What are you writing?" John asked, focused on his chessboard.

"A letter to Nana and Grandpa. Telling them a little about our life here."

He looked up and smiled.

"That's cool," he said.

THE NEXT MORNING there was snow on the ground and more pouring out of the sky. Without waiting for breakfast, David and John ran outside, John to drag in firewood and David to check on the horses and the goat. When they came back into the kitchen, their clothes were wet. Sarah was pulling muffins out of the oven. She poured the tea.

"Horses okay?" she asked, handing John a towel for his wet hair.

"They're fine," David said. His injured hand was bandaged and he held it out away from his body. He said he had slammed it in a fast closing gate at Seamus and Dierdre's. It reminded Sarah that there were so many ways to get hurt these days and without antibiotics or even topical ointments, the simplest cut could become infected.

"What about the sheep?" John asked. "They'll freeze to death out there."

David took a hot muffin and sat down at the kitchen table.

"Dierdre said they'll be fine. They're all wearing wool coats, you know. But we'll check on them later to make sure they're good."

That appeared to satisfy John. He wolfed down two muffins and a mug of tea.

"What about the chickens?" Sarah asked.

David and John had created a makeshift coop for the three chickens and one rooster given to them by Dierdre and Seamus. They hitched one of the horses up to a rudimentary harness and dragged a large piece of useless and rusting farm equipment out of what looked like a small barnyard shed. They prepared the inside as Dierdre had suggested with bedding and pine shavings on the floor. At the time, Sarah had watched them work together and felt her heart lift at their obvious closeness and the sounds of their voices and laughter.

"Dierdre said they should be fine in their coop for the winter," David said.

"I had no idea it would snow this early in Ireland." Sarah said.

"Dierdre said people are leaving the area."

"What do you mean? They're leaving Balinagh? Why? Is it better in the cities?"

"I guess they think so. Or maybe they're just moving to be closer to family. I mean, look at us, here. It's really hard just making breakfast happen. Most people wouldn't live like this if they had a choice."

"I don't like the feeling of being out here by ourselves."

John hopped up from the table.

"I'm tacking up Star," he said, pulling on his jacket. "Gonna check on the sheep in the far pasture."

Sarah frowned. *Give it to God Give it to God Give it...*She looked at David.

"Yeah, okay, I'll go with him," he said, shivering in anticipation of the cold. "Wait up, sport." But John was already gone.

"It *is* hard here," Sarah said.

"Yeah," David said. "But unlike everyone else, *we* don't have a choice."

He pulled on his jacket and one glove, tucked another muffin into his pocket and followed his son to the barn.

Sarah put the dishes in the sink and punched down the dough for the bread she was planning for lunch. She was going to serve up the goat butter she had made earlier.

John was right. They were all going to get rickets.

An hour later, she wandered out to the barn to pat a few horses' noses. It made her feel more confident the more she was around them. She picked up the chicken feed bowl and visited the coop first. The three chickens were huddled on their perches eyeing her.

She tossed them a spray of seeds which they ignored. She looked around for the rooster. He was probably strutting around outside somewhere. She felt under each hen and brought away two eggs which she tucked into the pocket of her jacket. She felt as proud as if she'd laid them herself. Fresh eggs meant a decent meal even if there was nothing in the rabbit traps today. She heard a noise behind her and whirled around. David stood in the door, cradling his hand to his chest.

"Oh, my God, you gave me a start," Sarah said, double checking that she hadn't broken the eggs.

"I saw the coop door opened and just wanted to make sure it

hadn't been left open accidentally," David said as they both moved out into the sunshine.

"Why aren't you with John? I thought you were going to check on him with the sheep."

"Sarah, he doesn't need me. He's fine." He held up his bandaged hand. "With this, it was more trouble than it was worth to get up on the horse. He didn't have the patience to wait and I didn't think it was necessary."

"This is not a safe place to be wandering about, David. I thought Dierdre made that clear to you." Sarah tried to fight down the surge of fear that began to radiate from her.

"We can't live like scared rabbits, either, Sarah."

"*Alive* scared rabbits," she said, suddenly furious with him. "He's barely ten. You let him do too much. And why didn't you tell me about the gun?"

"I thought you'd do pretty much what you're doing right now. You tend to be jittery. I didn't want to add to your anxiety."

The arrogance of him thinking he was less anxious than she was! Sarah was a second away from cracking one of the eggs on his head when they both heard the staccato pounding of the pony's hooves on the hard packed dirt road behind them.

"He's back," David said, frowning, as he looked over her shoulder.

Sarah emerged into the light to see John ride up to them, wheel his pony around and slide to the ground. His hair was wild and blowing, his eyes huge and his cheeks red from the cold.

"Dad! You gotta come!"

Sarah grabbed his arm. "What is it? What's happened?"

"It's the sheep. Something's got at 'em," John said, his eyes wild and darting from parent to parent. "One of 'em's...one of 'em got killed." Her son looked like he might cry and Sarah felt her stomach tighten.

"Okay, son, show me," David said heading toward the barn to

saddle Rocky. John shoved his pony's reins at Sarah and ran after this father.

Sarah stood there with the two eggs in her pocket and the pony's reins in her hands. She watched them enter the barn and wondered when it was that John had stopped wearing his hard hat.

9

"Why, exactly, do you have to spend the night out there?" Sarah asked David in frustration.

"Because if I don't John will do it and I'm sure you don't want him out all night armed with a rifle waiting for sheep killers to show up. Besides, he's right. We have to protect the sheep."

David was mounted on Rocky. Sarah handed him the rifle and a small bag of cold biscuits.

"So you're going to keep doing this from now on? Are a few sweaters really worth it? Because I thought we agreed the sheep aren't really of value to us beyond their wool."

"Look, Sarah, I don't know what their value is to us. But if we have to end up eating every fluffy one of 'em or starve to death come January, I'll be glad I didn't throw them away in October."

The one dead sheep looked to David as if it had been killed by a wild animal, so he mentally checked starving neighbors off the list of suspects. Even so, the flock needed protection.

That first night, he loosened Rocky's girth and tethered him to a bush. Next time, he decided, he would leave the horse behind and just walk the two miles to the pasture. The flock had found a natural stone windbreak and had bedded down nearby.

The spot where the single sheep had been attacked was still evident but it didn't seem to bother the flock. They grazed carelessly around the area which was still stained dark with the victim's blood.

David settled down on a blanket on the ground. He put the gun beside him.

This was nuts beyond believable, he thought. *I'm sitting in a pasture at night with a gun protecting a flock of sheep. My flock of sheep, in fact.*

He stared up into the autumn night sky and saw the stars so clearly he thought for a minute he must be hallucinating. He pulled a blanket over his shoulders and shivered.

A wave of sleepiness pushed over him and he leaned back against the stacked stones that served as the windbreak. He figured it was safe to sleep. If the sheep didn't wake him, Rocky surely would if someone or something was creeping about. He felt in his pocket for one of the biscuits. The grease from the goat butter coated his fingers and he licked them clean.

He appreciated that Sarah seemed to jump right in and figure out the skills they needed to help them survive. That was a part of her that didn't surprise him at all. He unwrapped one of the biscuits and bit into it. In their old life, she was always so together. No matter what life threw at them, she dealt with it. He'd gotten used to that.

On the other hand, he knew her ability to function came at a price. She took anti-anxiety medication to help her control what she insisted was a rational but constant fear. She said it had to do with a parent's normal concern for her child's safety, but really, in his opinion, it was a fear of just about everything.

He finished the biscuit and wiped his fingers on his jeans. He had to admit there was a lot to be afraid of nowadays. Even Dierdre was scared and she was the toughest lady he knew. He was grateful that Sarah seemed to be keeping it together in the face of this new, terrible situation they were all in. His worry now, now that she really *did* have something to be afraid of was a simple one:

How was she going to handle things when her meds ran out?

He remembered for a moment the woman he had fallen in love with so many years ago. Sarah had been downright fearless in those days.

It's a terrible thing to realize the person you thought you knew was just a cover for the person they really were. He wondered if she thought that about him. Had he changed since they'd come to Ireland? It was only four weeks now but he had callouses he never imagined owning. He closed his eyes. And here he was sitting out in the middle of a pasture a hundred miles from nowhere in the middle of the frigging night, waiting to shoot someone for messing with his sheep. Yeah, not in a million years could he ever have imagined *that* scenario back home. And David found himself smiling as he dropped off to sleep.

"WHOA, DAD," John said, "you're a heavy sleeper. What if I was a wolf or something?"

David woke to the sight of his son walking toward him and leading his pony. It was daylight. David yawned and stretched, instantly feeling every rock and stick that had dug into his back and hips while he'd slept.

"Hey, John. I don't suppose you brought a thermos of coffee?"

John started counting the sheep.

"They're all there," David said, getting up and picking up his blanket. "Rocky was my early warning device and he didn't go off all night so I know they're fine."

"Mom says breakfast is ready. I'll take over now."

David packed his saddlebag and tightened Rocky's girth.

"I don't think predators will attack in the daylight," David said.

John frowned. "Is that true? They only attack at night?"

David realized he had no idea.

"Yep. Only at night. Don't stay out too long, okay, sport? I'm going home to catch some shut-eye."

"I'll be fine," John said. He gave the gun a glance as David mounted with it.

"You don't need the gun. Something comes, throw rocks at it or come get me."

"Fine," John muttered.

BACK AT THE COTTAGE, a hot breakfast of scrambled eggs, biscuits and tea awaited him. And something else.

"Eat fast," Sarah said when he'd peeled off his jacket and sat down to his breakfast. "We don't know how long he'll be gone."

David had a forkful halfway to his mouth before he realized what she was saying. He bolted his food, grabbed a quick slurp of tea and met his wife in the corner of the cottage that served as their bedroom.

It had been over seven weeks since they'd touched each other in any kind of intimate way.

LATER, Sarah did the dishes and let David sleep. It was raining again, turning the thin layer of snow on the ground to slush. She realized she didn't even care about the rain, anymore. It didn't affect her intention one bit to tack up Dan and go keep John company in the north pasture. She tried to think of even one time she had been rained on back in the States. She'd always moved from house garage to car to office parking garage. She never even owned an umbrella. She didn't need to. She never got wet.

Sarah realized as she mounted Dan and moved out of the

frontcourt of the house that she had felt no anxiety tacking up the horse. She tried to remember when that had stopped. She leaned down and patted him on the neck. Probably about the hundredth time that she'd moved him out of the stall to clean up after him, or transferred him from barn to paddock. She was halfway to the pasture before she'd realized she was wearing only a thick wool knitted cap for protection against a fall. She'd left her own hardhat in the barn.

She never brought Dan out of a walk, just felt the peaceful rhythm of his gait through her hips and kept her eyes anywhere but on his feet. She left the road after fifteen minutes and let him pick his way through the snowy pasture. *Trust that he knows what he's doing*, she thought. She watched the birds, the horizon of grey clouds that looked like more snow was on the way.

The air was crisp and mean against the exposed portion of her face, but it also made her feel alive. She listened intently for any sound of her boy and his flock. As she got closer, a sensation like nervousness tingled in her chest until she realized it was joyful anticipation.

The world around her was beautiful and she was a part of it. She could see John from the top of the little hill she had just climbed. He sat on his pony as still as a statue, watching the flock and scanning the surrounding scrub and pasture. When he saw her, his hand went up in a wave and he began to move toward her.

"Did you bring the gun?" he asked.

"No, why?"

"I found the culprit," John twisted in his saddle and waved his hand to indicate that the animal was somewhere behind him. "A dog. He looks starved. We're gonna have to shoot him."

Sarah gaped at him. Was her own ten year-old son suggesting they kill a dog?

"Are you serious?"

"About what? That a dog's killing the sheep?"

"No, about wanting to kill the dog."

"Mom," John sounded like he was world-weary having to explain something so basic as his reasoning to her. "I don't *want* to kill the dog. I want the *sheep* to not get eaten."

"Maybe we could catch the dog," she said.

"So he can eat our chickens? Or Lucy?" (He'd named the goat.) "Miz McClenny says once a dog's eaten a chicken or a sheep, he can't unlearn the wanting for them."

Sarah felt a wave of exhaustion.

Why do we have to go through this? Why does my child have to even consider killing an animal we've taught him to consider a pet? Why does everything have to be so hard?

"Dad will do it," she said. "If you're sure it's the dog."

"Saw him with blood on his face. Saw him stalking the flock."

"Okay. Let's let Dad sleep a little longer. We'll stand guard on the flock in the meantime. Unless you're cold and want to, you know—"

"I'm good."

Sarah looked at the sheep. *They're oblivious. Danger is so close and they don't know. They're too stupid to be afraid.* Then she looked at John and watched him as he continued to scan the horizon, the brush and the rest of the pasture.

Suddenly, she spotted the dog but not before John launched a handful of rocks at it. Sarah watched the dog retreat—but reluctantly, she thought. It looked like someone's pet. Not a dingo or something wild. Just something hungry and desperate.

Like us.

SARAH FILLED her jacket pockets with the small heavy rocks John had collected and then sent him back to the cottage to fetch his dad and the gun.

"And don't come back with him," she told him. "Grab a bite to eat and feed Star. You don't need to see this."

"Mom, I saw *Old Yeller*." But she could see he didn't want to argue the point.

Later that evening, David returned from the pasture. Sarah couldn't remember ever seeing him look so tired. She and John had heard the rifle report an hour earlier. John hadn't looked up from the saddle he was trying to mend, but she could see he had registered the shot.

She and John met David in the frontcourt. David tossed his reins to John.

"Put him to bed for the night, will you, sport? Your old man's beat."

Sarah put her hand on David's sleeve and then jerked it back. Something was moving in the knapsack he had used to store the gun.

"Oh, yeah, there's this," David said, widening the neck of the sack.

"Puppies!" John cried out, with laughter in his voice. Sarah tried to remember the last time she had heard that happy childish tone come out of his mouth.

"Their mother was just trying to feed them," David said as he pulled out two black Labrador-mix puppies.

"You killed...you had to..." John said.

"Yeah, you were right, sport. She would've been impossible to rehabilitate. Sorry. But then I found these little guys. They're starving."

"Not for long," Sarah said fiercely. She gathered up the dogs in her arms and spoke to John. "Hurry with Rocky, and then come help me, okay? I've got some goat milk in the house."

John ran to the barn with the big horse.

"There were three," David said tiredly. "One died on the way back. I parked it under a stone out there."

"Oh, David."

"A real survivalist would've strangled them all. The last thing we need is more critters to feed."

Sarah reached up on tiptoe and kissed him.

"We're not savages yet. You turned a bad day into a sort of miracle."

He drew an arm around her as they walked back to the house, their earlier closeness coming back to both of them like a strengthening shield.

"Now, if we can just turn some bags of sawdust into a rump roast, I'll be good," he said.

FINN SAT in the trailer across the table from his brother and one of the bowsies who followed him without question. He smiled at the thought. *That would be just about everyone.* He shuffled the cards and dealt them out to the pockmarked gypsy he knew for a fact he shared a mother with.

He had a plan, a bloody, wonderful plan.

It might not work as well for the *culchies* around here who knew him or the rest of his so called family but it would work a charm for everyone else. Especially now, with all that's happened. It wasn't just him and his kind feeling the lack but everyone. That evened things up some. They'd all feel more agreeable to opening their doors to a rag-tag group of *survivors* than they would a lying, thieving gang of gypsy hoodlums.

Finn found himself chuckling and his brother looked up from his cards with a worried look on his face. Finn grinned at the bowsie and then his brother. He knew he would win the hand and the one after that. He knew they *let* him win. It was one of the perks of rank.

Might not even need to use force at first, he thought, laying down his winning hand on the table. At least not with the ones who didn't know him. But then, need and want were two very different things.

Didn't he, of all people, know that, if nothing else?

10

Sarah glanced at the words she'd written on the page.

Then once I actually get off the horse, my older body creaking like it will never limber up again, I'm not done yet. Instead of going inside to relax, I have to tend to the animals. Even if I've got blisters or aches or desperately have to go to the bathroom! In a way, it's sort of marvelous to learn that you can't control every movement of your schedule according to your whims. It's particularly marvelous for your grandson to learn that lesson now, at his age.

Just as I can no longer automatically control my comfort level by flipping on an air conditioning switch, I can't just park my transportation in the garage and get on with the next thing on my to do list. My transportation needs untacking, rubbing down, feeding and releasing into the paddock. That's if he doesn't step on me or poop somewhere I have to clean up first!

David's grandfather used to tell David that when he was a boy he always said "no" to one thing every day. I guess that's a concept that seems insane in today's America. But maybe it has value in this new life of ours. I'm glad to see John already understands how to do it. Me, I'm still trying to learn.

Will write again later. I cannot tell you what a day I have ahead of me!

Sarah put down her pen and flexed her fingers. The house was quiet. David had spent the night again at Dierdre and Seamus's. Sometimes he ended up working so late he just stayed late. Unlike the first time it happened, Sarah had learned to hold off on the panic attack until noon the next day when she would inevitably see him riding over the rise.

Outside it was as dark as night could be, yet Sarah knew her workday had begun. As soon as she lit the cook stove and boiled the water for their tea, she knew John would begin to stir.

They were two months into their new life.

THEY HADN'T SEEN anybody now for nearly three weeks. As Dierdre had predicted, the village of Balinagh had virtually emptied. The store and all of the other shops were boarded up. The cottages on the perimeter of the town were empty as well. Dierdre said she thought they were the only inhabitants left in all of western Ireland. While there was no way to know for certain, the thought made Sarah feel strangely safer.

If they wanted news, as unreliable as it was, they would need to travel to Draenago for it—an impossible twenty miles further south. Sometimes they saw people traveling on the road looking like they had all their belongings with them. Sometimes people actually showed up in their frontcourt asking for food or news.

John had gotten the idea to spell out "U.S.A." in white stones on the upper pasture so that when the rescue helicopter finally came for them, someone would know there were Americans living there. Sarah and David had exchanged a look when John had suggested it but didn't discourage him.

Life had fallen into a steady routine. John knew what he needed to do on his end: bait the rabbit trap; groom and feed the horses, goats and chickens; count and move the sheep; try to train the puppies. At night he repaired and cleaned tack, memorized Latin and French from a textbook they'd found in the cottage and taught himself chess gambits. The rest of his time was spent exploring the Irish countryside on horseback and watching the sky for the helicopter he knew was coming.

David went to Seamus and Dierdre's at least once a week and usually twice. He always came back exhausted but arms full of preserves or late fall garden harvest and instructions from Dierdre to Sarah—on how to weave, the best place to dig for peat, and better ways to make goat cheese.

When David was at home, he checked the rabbit traps, gutted and skinned the rabbits, cleaned the stalls, and constantly checked or mended the security of the doors and fence. With John, he had created a movable chicken pen that allowed the birds to spend every day on a fresh patch of grass. With effort, it could be moved with both of them dragging it. On the days that David was gone, John would hook the coop up to his pony and move it by himself.

For Sarah, her day began before it was light out. If she had yeast she made muffins or if not biscuits. She kept the cottage spotless—not easy to do with so much of their lives happening outside in the dirt and the wind. She cleaned and mended their clothes. She kept an inventory of the food cellar and made careful plans for their future meals. She milked the little goat daily and made bread dough every other day.

Evenings, she knit or read aloud. Sometimes she tested John on his Latin or French vocabulary. And she rode Dan a little bit— even if it was only in the paddock—every afternoon, rain or shine.

There was snow on the ground this particular morning and Sarah was glad David had not tried to come home the night before. The sun was up and made mesmerizing sparkles on the snow. She began the ritual of starting a fire in the cookstove.

She couldn't help but think *any day now*. She had to believe that every day took them closer to the day they would be rescued or when news would come that life had returned to normal. She slid the pan of biscuits into the oven and closed the door, appreciating the brief blast of heat. The only thing she knew for sure was that it was early November and winter was on its way.

She had decided to make a special meal for David's homecoming. She had been exchanging notes with Dierdre on how to kill and clean one of the chickens. There were eight now and they could afford to lose one to a meal. Besides, it had been several days since John's rabbit trap had been fruitful and they were all getting tired of biscuits and canned beans.

From the beginning, Sarah had worked to try not to see the birds as pets. It was hard. When she fed them, they now rushed to greet her. They gave her the precious eggs that made life so much more bearable. The thought of killing one of the "girls" was difficult. But for a week or more now, she had begun to see the challenge as an important step to her being able to provide for her family.

They all had to do difficult things in this new life. Looking at their animals as sources of food rather than affection was a new way of framing her worldview that Sarah was determined to master.

John came to the breakfast table and sat down. He looked half asleep.

"'Morning, sweetie." She set his mug of tea down on the table.

"Is this the day you gonna kill Ethel?" John yawned.

Is the child a mind reader?

"You...you named the chickens?" she asked.

He sipped his tea and then grinned.

"Just kidding. That would be dumb, naming chickens. Which reminds me..." He bolted away from the kitchen table and flung open the bathroom door where the puppies had spent the night. They were growing bigger. He led them at a run to the front door and flung it open.

"Out! Out!" he said. Then turned and went back to the bathroom, closing the door behind him.

Sarah smiled. She watched the puppies from the kitchen window. Whether from their horrific first few weeks in the world or the breed, they were a quiet and sweet couple of dogs. John had named them Patrick and Spongy. They followed him throughout his day. As soon as she was sure they wouldn't foul the bed sheets, she would let them sleep in the bed with them.

John collected the dogs from outside and returned to the table.

"Did you wash your hands?"

"What's the point? It's the one part of me that's always clean."

"John..."

Grinning, he hopped up and went to the kitchen sink to wash.

"So when are you gonna do it?" He asked over his shoulder.

Sarah took the biscuits out of the oven and slid one onto a small plate for him. She pried the biscuit open and put a sliver of goat butter and a dollop of one of Dierdre's blackberry preserves on it. Then she added a large scoop of scrambled eggs to the plate.

"As soon as possible. I want to get it over with. Besides, Dad'll be home by lunch which is when I'd like to...you know..."

"Serve her?"

She made a face that made him laugh. He pulled off two pieces of biscuit and fed them to his dogs.

"Gosh, Mom. Is this egg one of Ethel's, do you think? 'Coz that's what I call giving to the bitter end." He laughed again.

Sarah wagged a spatula at him that just made them both laugh harder.

DAVID PULLED off his sweatshirt in spite of the dropping temperatures. He'd been steadily sweating most of the day.

Seamus and Dierdre's farm was small by any standard, but it

was still more than the couple could handle, and now with Seamus less than capable, the place—once surely as pretty as any postcard farm in Ireland—was falling down from neglect.

David had slept until five that morning, awakened by the rain on the farmhouse's hard metal roof and the realization that he would be working in the mud and the rain all day.

Where's the quaint thatched roof when you need it? he thought, already tired before the day had even begun. As he pulled on his rubber boots and rubbed the sleep out of his eyes, Dierdre tiptoed into the living room and set a large mug of coffee in front of him.

"Breakfast in a tick," she whispered.

Wondering why she was whispering since he was clearly awake and he could see that Seamus was already moving about, David stood up and stretched the kinks out of his back. Could he ever have imagined *back home* that he'd awake to spend a full day in the kind of conditions he expected to be in today?

He pulled back a corner of one of the curtains in the front room and peered out into the grey gloom of a rainy Irish morning in late October.

He wondered how Sarah's parents were doing. His own folks had passed away nearly a decade ago—the tragic victims of a drunk driver on a country road. He had become very close to Sarah's mother and father, in many ways even closer than to his own when they were alive. He tried to imagine the chaos at home and how his in-laws might be faring. Would the neighbors help them? He prayed they would. It surprised him a little to realize that, lately, he'd done quite a lot of praying.

"We'll just be needing the cows milked," Dierdre said standing at the kitchen table where David could see Seamus was now seated. "And maybe just a few odd jobs."

David nodded and joined Seamus at the table. The rain looked worse from the kitchen window.

Man, it was really coming down.

David smiled at Seamus. "Morning, Seamus."

The old man looked at him blankly over his morning cup of tea.

BY NOON, David had brought the cows in from the pasture—a pool of mud and water—and cleaned their tails and hooves of the muck and filth they'd slept in and then walked through. He had milked them, fed them, and returned them to the pasture. He had groomed, fed and released the couple's pony into the paddock when the rain started to let up; repaired a hole in the wood and wire fence on the north section of the farm; fed the chickens, careful not to lose any; and raked the yard. Seamus had toddled along behind him like some present but witless supervisor.

He hated to leave Sarah and John alone so much but Seamus and Dierdre needed him. Sarah seemed to be handling it better than he could ever have imagined. Back home, to be honest, she vacillated between being a total basketcase about the most mundane things to somewhat of a control-freak. If he hadn't been married to her, he wouldn't have thought it possible for one person to be both.

Frankly, it wasn't the most pleasant way to live.

When he waved to Dierdre as she hung out laundry in the cold, wet weather, he felt an insistent ache run down both arms. Was all this just another case of him not being able to say no? Surely not. This was a world crisis needing everyone to pitch in and help each other. Back home, he had developed a reputation at work—a running gag, really—for being so accommodating that he invariably ended up doing his colleagues' donkey work as well as his own.

He watched Seamus tamp down the tobacco in his pipe and gaze, unseeing, to the horizon. It suddenly occurred to him that the two farms would do better to consolidate. The thought surprised him but as it took hold, it gave him strength and purpose. He would give Dierdre a little more time to come to the same conclusion herself and make the invitation and if she didn't, he'd suggest it. It made more sense for Sarah and John and himself to move in with Dierdre and Seamus, rather than the other way around. This was a semi-working farm with livestock and a garden, not a barely furnished tourist rental, although where they'd sleep he didn't have a clue. Buoyed by the idea, and with the sun struggling to make an appearance behind the clouds, David energetically washed the couple's pony gig. He had failed to drag it into the barn after the couple had returned to the farm the night before and the leather seat and tires were sodden and splashed with mud.

Before he took his first bite of the lunch Dierdre had prepared for him—with yet another pot of tea to wash it all down with—David wanted nothing more than to fall face first into the couch and sleep until morning.

And he still had a full afternoon's chores to do.

Sarah's morning had not gone well.

First, it had rained like it would never stop, forcing John to spend a good part of the morning indoors—never ideal for parent or child. Then, Ethel acted like she had prior Intel about the afternoon's planned activities. From the moment Sarah came into the coop, the chicken ran from her. And because she ran, the other chickens became afraid and ran, too. After fifteen minutes of stirring up more feathers and dust than a down pillow factory explosion Sarah grabbed the chicken and stuffed her in a pillowcase.

Now she was sweating and nearly as upset as the chicken. She backed out of the coop, glad that John had gone to the sheep pasture. All laughter aside, this was upsetting in anyone's book. She hurried with her squirming, thrashing bag of chicken hysteria to the area behind the barn that she'd already designated as the killing ground.

Dierdre had told her it would all go much better if she was fast and sure about what she was doing. Assuming she'd already pretty much botched *that* tactic, Sarah took a moment to try to calm her nerves. The bag twitched and convulsed maniacally at the end of her arm.

Be at peace now, she chanted inside her head. *There is nothing more intimate than the taking of a life for the purpose of sustenance. Oh, this is nonsense.*

She felt for the chicken's neck through the bag and hoping she didn't mistake it for a leg, twisted it. The adrenalin pumped through her when she wrenched as hard as she could.

The motion in the bag slowed and then stopped. Bright red blood began to seep out around her hands. Afraid for a moment that she'd literally torn the bird's head off, Sarah dropped the bag in the snow, turned and retched up her morning tea. She sat down with a hard thump beside the now still bag and burst into tears.

DAVID EXAMINED the broken fence by the eastern pasture. The three cows grazed peacefully nearby. Seamus' dog lay dead in the ditch.

How had he missed this, this morning?

Had the fence been deliberately broken? And if whoever had broken into the gate to steal a cow, why were they all still there? It would've made sense to butcher the cow in the pasture rather than try to steal it on the hoof—considering the speed at which cows move. The dog had its neck slit. *Why would someone kill a dog? Were they trying to take out the couple's alarm system? Was it just an act of senseless violence?* David shook his head and looked at Seamus who stared out across the pasture.

"Sorry about this, Seamus. Did you hear him bark at all last night?"

Seamus said nothing.

David looked at the cows, then back at the dog. He hadn't heard anything himself, but he had been so exhausted that his sleep had been more like a coma than a slumber. The dog, if he had barked, would not have awakened him.

"Dierdre will know," the old man said.

David nodded and turned to head back to the house.

"I'll get the shovel." It didn't look like he would be going home early today after all. He felt a wave of weariness and disappointment.

SARAH PULLED the roast chicken out of the oven and set it on top of the cook stove. She had enough potatoes and garlic and wild rosemary to make a proper feast of the dish. She was out of yeast but David seemed to prefer the simple flour biscuits anyway. The aroma from the chicken dish nearly brought tears to her eyes. Never had she been more proud of a simple roast chicken.

She looked out the kitchen window with the hope that she'd catch a glimpse of him coming down the main road on Rocky. She frowned. It was after three and she had expected him hours ago.

Out in the courtyard, she watched John as he put his dogs through their paces. He made them both sit and stay and then released them with little bits of muffin he had saved from his lunch.

She tapped on the window and he looked up.

"Let me know when you see Dad, okay?" she shouted.

He gave a thumbs up to indicate he understood and turned back to his training.

Sarah sat down with a cup of tea. She noticed a single chicken feather wafting alone in the corner of the room. The plucking and gutting had been nearly as traumatic as the killing. But the thrill of her accomplishment blotted out the pain and horror of the day. She looked at her beautiful golden brown roast, shiny with herbs and basted with goat butter.

A perfect, welcome home meal, she thought with a smile. She stood up to look out the window again.

FOUR HOURS LATER, she and John finished their dinner alone. The anxiety in the pit of her stomach had made it impossible to enjoy a single bite. Even John looked worried.

"Do you think something happened to him on the road?" he asked.

"I'm sure Dierdre and Seamus just needed him tonight," she said, not at all sure.

"It's just that it's not like Dierdre to keep him two nights in a row," John said. He walked to the front door and looked out down the road. "They know we need him, too."

Sarah knew he was right. Dierdre would have insisted that David come home tonight.

"He's been this late before," she said.

"No, he hasn't. Not ever."

"I'm sure he's fine."

"Based on what?"

"John, did you do a last check on the animals?"

He turned back to her. "Not yet," he said.

"Well, why don't you? I'll clean up here and we'll play a game of chess before bed."

"You're terrible at chess," he said, pulling on his coat.

"Well, you can read a book at the same time," she said with a grin.

He left the dogs with her. As docile as the puppies were, they were still too undisciplined to be around the horses for long without having to dodge a well-deserved kick.

Sarah went to the front door herself, as if watching the front drive would make David come, then turned and put away the roast chicken and leftover potatoes. Even without electricity, the refrigerator served as a fairly successful icebox. They kept milk bottles parked out on the porch all night but meat couldn't be left out without attracting animals. She wiped down the counters and wrapped the biscuits in wax paper to save for their breakfast.

It occurred to her that she had stopped taking her anti-anxiety medicine weeks ago. Funny. She had dreaded the day when she would take her last pill. Probably got more worked up about *that* than was rational. And then, things got so busy, she actually forgot to take them. She must have a week's supply left in her suitcase.

The real shocker was that, as relentlessly afraid as she was these days—for herself, for her husband, her son, for her parents back in the States—Sarah realized she didn't feel *that* different without the pills. The thought stopped her.

How could that be? she wondered.

All at once, both dogs stopped playing with the rag they were tugging on. They stood in the kitchen, the hackles on their backs rising, slow menacing growls emanating from them.

Sarah's hand froze as she was wrapping the biscuits and stared at the dogs.

In the next second, a horse's terrified scream punched the air outside the cottage. Sarah dropped the biscuits and bolted for the front door and the source of the noise.

It was coming from the barn.

11

Three men stood with their backs to her in the courtyard between the house and the barn. John stood between them and the barn. One of the horses in the barn screamed again. Sarah couldn't hear what the men were saying over the blood pounding in her own ears and the sounds of the horse.

As she approached, she saw John's eyes flick to her and then back at them, but it was enough to alert the men. They turned, almost as one. As soon as they turned, John disappeared into the barn.

Sarah stood with the rifle to her shoulder and aimed at them.

"We're just hungry, missus,"

Three men, two rounds, she thought. *No warning shots.*

"Leave us," she said hoarsely. "Go away."

They looked like what she would expect men to look like who'd roamed the countryside, slept in ditches and stolen or killed to keep themselves fed. They looked dangerous, desperate and aggressive. Their faces were filthy and bearded, their eyes glazed. One man took a step toward her and she shifted her aim toward him.

"Give us the horses and we'll let you be," the man behind him said. Sarah dared not take her eyes off the man in her sights. She knew she should be taking the measure of the speaker. Clearly, he was the leader. She felt a twinge of gratitude that John had disappeared.

"You'd better get out of here," Sarah said, aware that her voice was coming from a place she didn't recognize.

The speaker laughed. "American?" he said. "I've seen the telly. She's American," he said to his companions.

Another man laughed. The one who'd stepped forward had not come any closer. He watched her eyes carefully and grinned at her through broken teeth.

Not caring that they could see what she was doing, Sarah dug into her pocket and fished out a third round. Her eyes never left the man in front of her.

"Oh, so you'll be needing to reload to dispatch the lot, eh?" The speaker laughed and slapped the man next to him. "She's got two chances, then she's done," he said. "You take 'er, I'll get the boy—"

The words weren't out of his mouth before Sarah shot him.

He screamed and grabbed his upper arm which instantly mushroomed red.

Sarah recovered quickly from the recoil and turned the gun on the nearest man to her when he suddenly made a strangling noise and pitched forward. When he went down, Sarah saw John standing behind him with a large manure shovel in his hands. She didn't waste the moment he'd given her.

She swiveled the gun barrel to the third man and, without taking her eyes off him, shoved another round into the rifle and slid the action forward. She repeated it with a third round. One man lay stunned at her feet, another stood hopping up and down and cursing while he clutched at his shoulder.

"I got one for each of you now," she said.

The unharmed man slowly raised his hands in surrender.

Sarah took a deep breath and felt the arm that held the gun begin to shake.

John approached with the shovel.

"Keep 'em covered, Mom," he said.

Sarah nodded, not trusting herself to speak. She took another deep breath. John turned to look at her and she gave him what she hoped he would interpret as a meaningful look. Then she spoke:

"John, you remember why we had to kill that dog that was savaging our sheep?"

John looked at the men. "It was because we couldn't trust it wouldn't return and kill more sheep."

"Sure, you're not thinking of killing us in cold blood, missus?" The man with his arms upraised looked from Sarah to the man who was bleeding. "Mack, you hear this maniac?"

"Desperate times call for desperate measures," Sarah said. "It's not personal."

The wounded man called Mack looked at Sarah, his face contorted with loathing. "You can't shoot us," he said.

"I'm protecting my family," Sarah said, feeling stronger every second. "I'll need you to stand away from the barn a bit. I don't want to have to drag bodies any further than I need to..."

The stunned man on the ground began to stir.

"You better get your buddy there to connect with the program, Gilligan," Sarah said, indicating the groaning man on the ground. "He makes me nervous."

"Georgie, wake up. Wake up, you stupid sod!"

"We're begging you, Missus. We never woulda hurt you and the lad. We're just hungry and—"

"You can't let 'em go, Mom," John said. "Maybe if you kill two of 'em, the third one will have learned a lesson."

Shrieks of horror burst from two of the men. The uninjured one howled the loudest. The leader, Mack, bleeding from his shoulder stared at her with an intense expression.

"That is a good idea, John," Sarah said. "But which ones?" She pointed with the rifle barrel at the one in the dirt.

"Yeah, that's good. And the one you shot will probably die anyway so he's a good second choice."

"It's a minor wound," Mack blurted, his eyes darting back and forth from Sarah to John.

"So are you saying she should kill *me* then, Mack?" The unharmed man said.

"Well, it's me that's led the band up to now, Ardan," Mack snarled.

"And got us in this mess, too, I'll be thinking," Ardan said. Suddenly, without warning, he wheeled on John who had walked too close to him and snatched him up. John never let go of the shovel and swung it in a wide arc, banging it into the head of the man with the wounded shoulder who screamed.

Sarah watched it as if she were watching a movie with the sound turned off. She saw the shovel smash into Mack's head and then drop uselessly from John's grip. She watched the man who held her son hesitate for a split second to react to his leader's scream of pain and in doing so dropped John to waist level.

That was her moment. She squeezed the trigger and shot him, straight and true, through the head. She never even felt the recoil.

She would remember John lurching away from the falling corpse, blood sprayed across the back of his jacket. He retrieved his shovel and stood, panting, next to Sarah.

She licked her lips, ignoring the body on the ground.

"I have two bullets left," she said, pointing the gun at Mack. "You and your buddy leave now before I change my mind."

HOURS LATER, David threw a tarp over the body and returned to the kitchen. He had ridden home, determined not to be separated another night from his family. On the road, he had seen two men stumbling in the dark. There was something about them that worried him and he reached down to touch the small hatchet he carried in his saddlebag. They passed him without a word and he cantered Rocky the rest of the way home.

"I didn't take time to think," Sarah said to David as he ate a late supper of cold chicken and John slept in the next room with a puppy on either side of him. "I just knew that at that range I couldn't miss."

David shook his head. "You didn't worry about hitting John?"

"I didn't have time to think about that. I just knew I had to stop it *now*."

David looked over his shoulder to where John slept.

"Do you think he's okay?"

"I don't know. We were joking about shooting them to scare them. And then all of a sudden it just happened. So I don't know."

"You were *joking* about killing them?"

"I didn't decide to execute that man, David," she said in a loud whisper. "He grabbed our son. He—" All of a sudden, Sarah got an image of the chicken in the burlap bag. She thought of how easy it had been to break its neck, all things considered.

"He could've killed John with his bare hands in just a moment," she said quietly. "So, no, I...I didn't think twice."

FINN'S PAIN mirrored his anger, climbing in arcs of intensity higher and higher, until he felt nearly incapable of speech. As he lay thrashing in his cot, his arm blazing in agony although the women had successfully staunched the blood, he thought for a moment he might literally lose his mind.

By the time he and Georgie had limped back to camp, he was delirious with pain and thoughts of revenge.

That bitch! He would kill her and the lad before breakfast and torch their miserable hut with their bodies inside!

After three months of steady, unfailing obedience from his followers, the disaster at the American's farm had shocked and destabilized him. He was so beside himself when he entered camp that he had been literally frothing in a wild fury.

Their first raid and he had made a bollocks of it. Or rather, Ardan had, and gotten himself killed in the process, the ejeet.

"What happened?" the girl Jules had asked as she bandaged up his arm. If he hadn't been so weak from the loss of blood, he would have backhanded her for suggesting the raid had been a cock-up. That moron Georgie babbled out a version of the story to probably the first attentive audience of his young, backward life.

"It went bad, so it did," Georgie kept saying to anyone who would listen. "And now they got Ardie, and him all dead and everything."

Jules had cried as secretly as she could manage when she heard about Ardan. Finn knew they were sweet on each other. It turned his stomach that his younger brother could make the girl smile—and more—*and hadn't he been so nice to her ever since he got back from the clink?*

It annoyed him to lose Ardan. He needed all the men he could gather for his plan of owning the surrounding countryside. Ardan was a pain in the arse, but he took orders well enough.

When Finn took a break from his own misery to notice Jules, he found himself comforted by the fact that there was a clear road to her now.

As if he wouldn't have gotten around to taking her from his brother eventually.

He put his hand out from where he lay on the cot. She was pretty, he thought, as if seeing her for the first time, even with tears on her cheeks and that scared-rabbit look in her eyes.

"Hush, lass," he said. He noticed she clamped her eyes shut as if to will the tears to stop, perhaps worried they were offensive to him.

"I know you loved Ardan," he said, forcing his voice to sound calm. "I loved him, too, so I did."

Her eyes popped open and he could see he had her. She slid her hand into his and he squeezed it.

"And we'll get the bitch did this to me...and him. And I promise ye that. In the name of all that is holy," Finn said. "We'll make her pay in the blood of every living thing she loves."

12

They needed more bullets.

And they desperately needed news.

Since the Crisis, Dierdre and Seamus had been getting all their information about the outside world from an old duffer named Devon O'Shay who lived on the edge of Balinagh and who used to stop in once a week for a meal.

For years he had driven to their place in his second hand Renault. When the Crisis happened, he came in his pony trap, pulled by an ancient polo pony that hadn't been ridden in a decade. Devon was an elderly widower who knew Seamus from their school days together in the Balinagh boys' school. His wife had been Dierdre's sister. Unlike Dierdre and Seamus who were childless, Devon and his wife had five children, all of them grown and gone and out of the country.

Devon hadn't visited in four weeks.

Sarah said, "So they assume something's happened to him." She fixed breakfast the morning after the gypsy men had come.

David nodded. "And they're worried but it's hard for them to get out. Seamus seems to be getting even foggier and Dierdre

knows it just takes one broken cart axel ten miles from home to...
you know."

Sarah stopped and looked at him. "Did Dierdre ask you to
check on him?"

"No, but you could tell she was really worried about him,
Sarah. Plus, when you think about it, Devon is their only source
of news of the outside world and so *our* only source."

"Sounds like you've talked yourself into going to look for
him." She turned her back to address the stove.

"There doesn't seem to be much harm in it," David said. He
had awoken hours before breakfast to drag the body out of sight.
He would spend the rest of the morning digging a trench for it.

David was still trying to process what had happened. The fact
that thugs had come to the house was bad enough. But knowing
that Sarah had shot and killed one? He still couldn't believe it.

Except for the body he now needed to bury.

"David." Sarah put down his plate of eggs and looked out the
kitchen window to catch sight of where John was. "You have
enough to do right here without finding an excuse to go
wandering about the Irish countryside. What more has to
happen to convince you that it is not safe here?"

"Look, Sarah..." He reached out to touch her but she pulled
away, refusing to be mollified. He hesitated and picked up his
fork instead. "We need news of what's going on. *I* need news."

"Fine. Then I'll go."

"You?"

"Look, David, I killed a man last night, okay? I think I can
handle it."

He noticed she was breathing fast. He stood up and took her
into his arms.

"Of course you can handle it. I just hate that you have to. I
wish I could protect you from all of this."

The kitchen door flew open and John entered, his hair wild
with the wind, his face flushed red from the cold.

"Awwww, mushy stuff," he said, plopping himself down at the kitchen table. "Are these for me?" He grabbed David's fork and began to eat his second breakfast of the day.

David grinned and released his wife. "They are now," he said.

Sarah broke three more eggs into a bowl and turned back to the stove.

LATER THAT MORNING David worked on the grave and John was on strict orders to stay in the house with the dogs. They did a practice run-through of John yelling from the kitchen window to see if David could hear him from behind the barn where he was digging.

No problem. David would keep the gun with him while he worked. John would keep all the doors and windows locked, with the kitchen window open so he could hear and be heard.

Sarah tacked up Dan. She carried a knife and two bottles of Côte de Rhône. She hoped to be able to trade the wine for ammunition or something else more useful to them.

Ballinagh was a little over nine miles to the west, which should take her about two hours at a walk. She fully intended to trot Dan most of the way home to cut her time. He could use the exercise and the light would be fading by then.

She and David decided she would ride straight to Balinagh. Devon had reported that some of the people who hadn't left the area were still in the habit of coming to the now deserted village to set up markets. Sarah's hope was that she would find a market and be able to trade her wine and pick up any news.

On the way back, she would swing by where David thought Devon's cottage was. This would only take her about a mile off her route. David was very serious in reinforcing to her that if she saw *anything at all* that looked dangerous or threatening, she was to bypass the place.

As Sarah rode away from the cottage, waving to her son and

husband, she wondered what that might look like. If it was totally quiet when she showed up, should she assume someone was waiting for her in ambush or that Devon was hurt and praying that help would arrive? If she saw activity in his front yard—dogs barking, or whatever—should she stop?

It occurred to her that if Devon's house looked like there was no trouble there, that wouldn't explain why he hadn't come to Seamus and Dierdre's in almost a month. She would just have to make a decision based on what she saw and hope it was the right one.

The ride to town was cold and although Sarah had volunteered for it—and thoroughly surprised herself in the process—she was pleased to note that the trip already felt like it was doing her good. She stretched out her legs on either side of Dan and relaxed her spine and when she did she could feel him relaxing, too. She held his reins loosely in her left hand and scanned the horizon for any movement or activity. It had been a full eight weeks since she'd been to the village and she wasn't at all sure what to expect when she arrived.

She realized that the decision to go, herself, was a good one. A part of her couldn't bear to have David leave so soon after being gone. She was surprised to realize the burden of protecting their cottage–and her son—was heavy. Every step that took her away from that terrible responsibility seemed to free her just a little. Or was it every step that took her away from the body of the man she had killed?

She had worked hard during the night not to think of it. She had alternately hugged her sleeping boy and her exhausted husband and put thoughts away of the man's eyes as he'd breathed his last—because of her.

She found other thoughts just as disquieting creep into her head, thoughts of wondering about his birth and boyhood. *Had his mother loved and cherished him just as she did John? Did he have children? If this crisis hadn't happened, would she have known him? Sat next to him in church?*

The brutal fact that she had extinguished him came upon her in moments without warning. Staring at the goat butter bubble in a hot pan; watching an arc of Roseate Terns swoop languidly over the snowy pasture; cleaning up after one of the dogs. And then his face would appear to her, his startled then glazed eyes, his blank face full of nothingness now.

At one point in the night, Sarah actually found herself thinking with amazement that he was lying out there in their courtyard when any sane person knew enough to find a place for warmth and shelter.

If you do it out of instinct, are you any less culpable? she wondered. There had been no decision, no thought process. She had simply reacted. And her reaction was an instantaneous action to strike someone from the list of the living.

She shook her head and took a long breath.

Dear God, who will I be when we finally make it back home?

THE TALL IRISHMAN hoisted himself into the back of the wooden wagon and raised his arms to the gathering crowd. He had deliberately parked the wagon near the center of the village square in Balinagh, waiting until the peak of trading and marketing had waned. He figured that would guarantee the attention of a maximum number of people but with fewer distractions to contend with since the heaviest drinking had yet to fully begin.

"If I could have your attention," he bellowed to the forty or so people milling about the wagon. "Your attention, if ye please."

"Oy!" A young ginger-haired youth stood next to the wagon and addressed the crowd. "A moment of your time." He looked up expectantly at the man standing in the back of the wagon.

The crowd, mostly men intent on moving from the trading

portion of their day to the drinking portion, hesitated and then began to walk toward the wagon.

Mike Donovan, satisfied he had their attention, lowered his arms but continued to speak loudly.

"You'll all be knowing me," he said. "I'm Michael Donovan from south of Killmilloch on the coast. I'm a fisherman and most of you know me for that but some of you also know me as a good neighbor. I'm known in Balinagh and Siobhan Scahill can attest to my character." He nodded in the direction of Siobhan's store off the main street.

"I'm talking to you today," he said, "because I'm thinking we need to come together as the community we are. Now me and my family are creating a group down by Killmilloch that's near the water—so's we can fish and provide for our families—and also farm. Now I know..." He raised his arm again and surveyed the crowd that was gathered around the wagon, "...farming's not been good to most of us in the last few years but I'm thinking that's going to change what with all that's happened and all. I'm inviting any and all who want to come and live with us—in the community we're trying to build—in Killmilloch. It'll be hard work, no mistake, but nobody knows how long any of this'll last..." He swung his arm to indicate the shuttered village street.

"With no laws nor government, there's plenty among us could use help and plenty able enough to give it. I believe there's strength in numbers and that together we can rebuild, come what may, no matter what mischief the Yanks or the bloody English have gotten us all into. And we'll live better together than apart. That's all I have to say and if you're interested, I hope you'll come talk to me."

A man called up to him: "Do you have housing for us, then, Mick?"

"It's Mike, and no, we have sheds and barns and strong backs to help those that can build houses."

"And food?" an elderly woman yelled out. "Do you have food in this Killmilloch of yours?"

"We have enough. And with more people working to farm and fish and help with the livestock, we'll have enough for everyone. If everyone pulls their weight, we can build a community that will take care of us all."

"Or we could just leave."

Mike and the crowd turned to the high-pitched woman's voice that came from the perimeter of the crowd. People parted as Siobhan made her way forward toward Mike's wagon.

"Everybody here knows Siobhan Scahill from Scahill's grocers," Mike said.

"We could just leave, Mike Donovan," Siobhan said. "And go to the towns that have food and laws still working."

"And where would that be, now?" Mike's hands rested on his hips as he addressed her. "Dublin? Limerick? London?"

Siobhan turned to the crowd.

"Why would you stay here? When there's nothing here but hunger and dried up farms?" She glanced up at Donovan. "Most of these farms haven't been worked in two decades. You know that. Are you really going to multiply the fishes to feed the masses? I think Father McGinty will take issue with *that*."

The crowd laughed and Mike saw a few of the men on the edge wander away, presumably in search of their jars.

"I don't believe in running away as the answer," he said.

"It is if there's nothing here," Siobhan said. "It is if the country is crawling with pikers and murderers and there's nothing to eat and no help coming."

"Which is why we need to band together to help ourselves," Mike said.

Siobhan addressed the crowd.

"I'm leaving Balinagh by the end of the week. Anybody wantin' me store, you're welcome to it." She turned to look at

Mike but spoke loudly to the people gathered. "I'll not be coming back," she said. "Whatever comes now."

BY THE TIME Sarah rode into the western entrance to Balinagh, her back felt limber, her seat relaxed and her rhythm totally in sync with Dan.

Twelve years ago she had given up trail riding for good. She had restricted herself to riding in the paddock or enclosed jumping arenas, carefully avoiding the jumps. The thought of going out into the pasture or on any of the trails—even with a group of other riders—had terrified her.

When a friend at the barn where she rode gently pointed out to her that there seemed to be little point in her perfecting her riding technique if she refused to actually ride anywhere other than the paddock, Sarah didn't have an answer. She knew what she was missing. She had trail ridden for years, and happily. She remembered the startled foxes and quail and the pleasures of the morning that could be seen only from horseback–the sunrise, the flowers, the birds, the smell of life, organic and exquisite. She knew what magic riding out in the world held. It was the reason she had begun riding in the first place.

She wasn't sure exactly when her confidence had eroded until it finally left her altogether. All things considered, her fall had been a gentle one. There was no blood, no splintered bones, just a clean snap and a matter-of-fact drive to the emergency room. She had even fed her horse and released him back into the pasture before allowing a friend to drive her to the hospital.

A broken shoulder, although inconvenient to her life outside riding, had not put her in a wheel chair or attached her to a colostomy bag. It had healed quickly and she had eagerly returned to ride. But, bit by bit, everything changed after that.

Before long she was running tapes in her head that she couldn't stop. The mental tapes varied from day to day—images of her horse throwing her and her body rolling down the barb-wire-lined ravines, images of the horse panicking and racing through the woods and the brambles while tree branches lacerated her.

The tapes ran in her head when she rode alone. So, she stopped riding alone. Then the tapes ran when she rode in the pasture or on the beautiful trails that wound up and around the Chattahoochee River near the barn where she boarded her horse. So she stopped going out on the trails.

Pretty soon, the tapes would start as soon as she swung up into the saddle. It was about that time that she met David and decided the courtship didn't allow time to include horses too. She sold her horse and put her tack up for sale on eBay.

As she approached the village Sarah realized with surprise that her focus was so keenly on what she would find there that the fact that she was riding alone in an unfamiliar rural surrounding had not even come to mind. She took in a big breath and let it out slowly as she felt her control of her horse, utterly and completely.

She patted his neck. She had always been afraid of big horses. Her own horse had been no bigger than a large polo pony, and was as docile and sweet as a golden retriever. Yet Sarah had practically given her away and had breathed a sigh of relief as if she had unloaded a demon on wheels.

Sarah tightened her calves against Dan's sides and he moved more quickly forward. She could see the village in the distance and that there *was* a market set up today.

The laughter and the music reached her before anything else. Sarah smiled. *The Irish and their music,* she thought. *Do not let an international disaster stand in the way of what's important.*

When she reached the mouth of the main street she could see about twenty tents and tables set up, all of them crowded with people. A fiddler, the source of the music, was established in the center in a makeshift stage. A large group crowded around, laughing and clapping and generally looking like they'd never seen a street performer before. A few people glanced at her as she rode Dan down the street. She could see a line of saddled horses off to the side, tied to a rope strung across the street. There were four pony traps still attached to the ponies.

She slid to the ground from her saddle and led Dan to the line of horses. A couple of people turned, watching her. She slipped the bit out of his mouth and pulled the bridle off Dan's face until it hung on his neck. Then she wrapped the reins in a loose knot on the tie-up line. She loosened his girth to the very last notch.

Someone tries to steal him, she thought, *they'll be doing it with a fifteen-pound saddle flopping around his stomach.* She pulled the wine bottles from the saddlebags and turned to join the crowd.

"IT'S NOT ME, YOU UNDERSTAND," the young woman said, dabbing at her eyes. "It's me children, sure they're so young and to see them so hungry..." She looked at Sarah and shook her head. "It's fair to killing me, so it is."

Sarah nodded her head in commiseration. The young woman had a problem, that was clear. Sarah wiped the grime from her hands. The mug of tea she held turned the moist dirt to a film. Her eyes flickered, for the millionth time, to where Dan was tied.

I killed a man, she thought, as she watched a man stagger to the line of horses, fish out his own horse, mount it with some difficulty and slowly jog away.

Yesterday.

The young woman spoke again.

"If your husband could see his way to helping me, I hate to ask. It's not for myself, you understand. It's for me little ones."

Sarah looked back at her. The market was winding down and she knew it was time for her to go, too. She still had to check in on Devon on the way home.

She had traded the two wine bottles within minutes of offering them up for nearly four hundred rounds. Her hand touched the package in her lap. But the big prize was the semiautomatic in which the rounds fit. A Glock 19 complete with shoulder holster. No safety, a relentless push of the trigger would empty fifteen rounds, a full magazine, one right after the other.

The woman who sold it to her had just lost her son but Sarah had not had the nerve to ask how. Her husband, a mute and somber man who stood at her side, knew the tourist cottage where Sarah lived. He would be by tomorrow to take the six sheep and dozen more bottles of Côte de Rhône Sarah had bartered in exchange for the gun.

She cleared her throat, put down the empty mug and stood up.

"I'll ask my husband," she said to the woman who sat, wringing a wet rag in her hands. "I'm sure he'll be able to help you."

"Oh, bless you, missus. What with losing my Jamie, I don't know how to thank you."

"The cow," Sarah said. "You said you'd trade one of your milk cows?"

"Aye, yes, sure. We have three, I'll not be needing more than one. But if your husband could come and dig out the well. Not more than a few days, probably just a day, him being American and so clever and all."

Sarah couldn't put her finger on why, but there was something about this girl that unsettled her.

"Where is your farm?" Sarah asked.

The young woman shook her head.

"Sure, it's impossible to describe the way. I can meet Himself right here, you just say when, and I'll lead him there. And I can't thank you too much. My children...it's just that when me husband, when Jamie..." she began to cry again and Sarah patted her on the shoulder.

"Don't worry, Julie," she said. "I'm sure David will be able to help you and your well. What time tomorrow can you be here?"

"You tell me," Julie said, smiling through her tears. "Sure, you tell me when and I'll be here."

Sarah would have preferred to have had at least one day with David before he was off again, but the young woman's need was urgent. The well at her farm had caved in and they had no fresh water. Her husband had been recently killed in a freak accident (on horseback) and she had two children under five depending on her. Sarah knew well the feeling of fear and desperation to protect her child. And the thought of having real milk on a regular basis nearly brought tears to Sarah's eyes.

"Noon tomorrow," she said, patting Julie's hand. "He'll be here."

AN HOUR LATER, Sarah stood next to her horse on a small rise and watched the front of the old stone cottage. It looked like it had been built in the fifteen century. If it hadn't been falling into disrepair, it would've qualified as a quaint little Irish tourist cottage, complete with thatched roof.

She had been standing there nearly fifteen minutes, wondering what it was she was seeing. It looked deserted. No smoke from the chimney and it was certainly cold enough to warrant a fire. She buttoned her jacket to her neck and inspected the sky. She had stayed in Balinagh too long. It would be well past dark by the time she got home.

No dogs barked to herald her presence. No smoke in the grate. Her eyes scanned the courtyard to see if there was a lifeless form laid out to explain all the other signs of lifelessness.

So this is where I decide, she thought, watching the cottage. *This is where I ride into an ambush or decide to play it safe and just go home.* She looked up again at the greying sky. Bad weather was moving in. She sighed and moved forward, leading her horse.

I can't not check on him, she thought. *It's why I came in the first place.*

She counted on her horse reacting first to any unseen threat in the forecourt or the perimeter of the cottage. She had loaded the handgun before she left the village. She walked slowly, the gun pressing reassuringly against her side in its shoulder holster. Directly in front of her, the cottage sat in front of a truncated drive. On its north side was a shed that had been transformed into a makeshift carport. As she approached, she could see the rear bumper of a car protruding from it. There was no sign of the pony.

She stopped in front of the cottage and scanned the windows for any sign of life. She had already rehearsed in her mind her escape route up the far drive on the other side of the carport. Somewhere off in the pasture, she heard a bird singing. She held her breath and waited. There was no other sound.

Still holding onto Dan's reins, she stepped up onto the cottage porch. Now she could see that the door was ajar. Making up her mind, she turned to Dan and swung up into the saddle. She touched the handle of the Glock for assurance and rode him down the drive to the other side of the car shed. She figured if there was anyone there, her action might flush them out for fear she was leaving.

She trotted down the side of the cottage, looking everywhere at once, stopping, listening. She returned to the frontcourt of the cottage and dismounted. She tied Dan to the porch railing, stepped onto the porch and pushed the front door the rest of the way open.

He was lying on the floor in front of the couch.

Sarah stepped over an overturned chair to the body. The cottage interior seemed to have been stripped of anything of value. She noticed a lone tea mug on the kitchen table. She knelt by the body and touched his neck, not sure whether she was looking for a pulse or just confirming that he was as cold as she knew he would be. The fading light through the window was strong enough to show that he had no visible wounds, no stabs or gunshot markings. Sarah looked around the cottage.

The smell was thick with decay.

There was nothing she could do for Devon now. It was at the moment that she turned to leave that the flutter of fear and anxiety returned to vibrate through her entire body.

It was also the moment she heard voices outside.

13

The man was very large and standing by her horse, inspecting the saddle and running a large hand down Dan's legs. Sarah stood motionless in the doorway and watched him, the gun in her hand but by her side. She waited for him to notice her or make a move. Unless he'd been talking to himself, voices meant there was another man nearby. Sarah focused on the big man, her *tactical environment*, and counted on her other senses to locate the second man.

The man by the horse saw her.

"Good day, missus," he said, moving away from Dan.

Sarah resisted the urge to point the gun at him.

"Can I help you?" she said.

Why do we Americans say that? she thought.

"Help me?" The man frowned, his eyes catching the glint of the Glock at the end of her arm.

"Are you looking for Devon?" she asked.

Where was the other guy? she wondered.

"Devon's dead, poor bugger."

"I know."

Well, obviously, I know that. I'm in his cottage.

"And you are...?"

"I'm a friend of Devon's sister-in-law."

"She's the American, Da." A younger man in his late teens came from the direction of the car shed. "The ones rented the McKinney's place, right?" He didn't smile but something about him didn't feel threatening to Sarah.

"That's right."

"So, you'll be knowing Dierdre?" The older man spoke again and Sarah felt the hand that held the gun relax a bit.

"She's my neighbor. She asked me to check on Devon. They hadn't seen him in awhile."

"Cor, she's got a pistol, Dad. You see that?" The younger man came closer, not taking his eyes off the gun in her hand but absent-mindedly patting Dan on the neck.

"I'm sorry," Sarah said. "I'm...I'm being careful."

"Too right," the older man said. "I'm Mike Donovan and this here's me son, Gavin. We've come to bury the old man. We mean you no harm, missus."

"I got the keys to his car, Dad. They were on the top shelf where he always kept 'em."

Donovan looked at Sarah.

"He'll not be needing the car," he said. "And we can trade its parts for food and supplies."

Sarah didn't care who took whose car. The light was fading fast and she needed to be mounted and on her way. From here, she could see by the open flaps that Donovan had examined the contents of her saddlebags, and knew she had a king's fortune in rifle and handgun rounds. She didn't dare take her eyes off him but she was tempted to look to see if they'd brought shovels, which would confirm his story.

"Fine," she said, not moving. "I'll let you get on with it."

The young man charged up the porch stairs and Sarah, startled, jerked her gun arm up.

"Whoa! Whoa! Gavin, you moron, she's got a gun, for Chrissake."

Gavin looked at Sarah with surprise and then turned to his father.

"I know, Da. But we need to…"

"Slowly, son. Let the woman get off the porch before you mow her down. I'm sorry, Missus," Donovan shoved a hand through his thick hair. Sarah looked for any guile in his eyes and thought she saw only weariness and anxiety.

"Gavin, get down here and let her pass," Donovan spoke slowly as if talking to a feeble-witted child.

Sarah would have preferred they both left or at least moved away but she realized there would be no other opportunity.

"I'm sorry," she said again. "I've had cause not to trust people recently." She shifted the gun to her other hand and wiped the perspiration from her palm on her jeans. She moved down the porch, her eyes never leaving Donovan's and, grabbing Dan's reins, jerked them free from the porch rail. The man touched his son's shoulder and motioned for him to move back a few steps and give her space.

If they were going to rush her, Sarah thought, the moment she attempted to mount would be the time. She knew she couldn't get up without tucking her gun away. Quickly, Sarah positioned Dan between herself and the two men, shoved the gun into her holster, grabbed the cantle, jammed her foot into the stirrup which was nearly as high as her waist and swung up in what seemed like slow motion.

Once in the saddle, she could see the men were patiently waiting for her. She left the gun where it was and gathered up the reins in both hands. Pulling back, she forced Dan to back up a few steps.

"Do you know how he died?" she asked, feeling more comfortable now that she was mounted *and* armed.

Donovan shook his head.

"Not at-tall," he said. "Maybe a heart attack? And then the hyenas came down to pick the bones." He waved a hand at the cottage. "Sure it doesn't look like foul play, just bad luck. I hope you'll be telling Dierdre that. Tell her Mike Donovan will make sure he's buried proper, so I will."

The light was nearly dusk but still Sarah lingered.

"How do you know Dierdre?" she asked.

"It's Seamus, really," Donovan said, turning and pulling a long handled shovel out of a ruck sack Sarah hadn't seen before. "He was me teacher. Well, everyone's. Did you not know he was the village schoolmaster? Everyone round these parts was schooled by Seamus at one time or another."

"I'm sorry, again, I'm sorry for..." Sarah indicated the porch.

Donovan waved her off.

"Not a-tall," he said. "These are times to be untrusting. You'd best get on where you're going. There'll be no moon tonight."

Sarah paused. She hated how she had acted. These were good people, doing a difficult job and she'd practically held them at gunpoint and, worse, nearly shot the boy. As she turned Dan to pick up the main road from Balinagh, she found herself vowing not to let whatever "these times" were turn her into something less than human.

MIKE WATCHED Sarah ride off and shook his head in amazement.

"How do you know about her?" he asked as he handed Gavin the shovel.

The boy shrugged. "It's all over town, isn't it? Being American and all."

"Is it just Herself?"

"No, there's a husband and a kid, too. Why?" He grinned at his father. "Took a fancy, did ya, Da? And her a pistol-packing Mama and all."

"Shirrup, ya ejeet," Mike said affably, pushing him in the direction of the backyard where the grave needed to be dug.

Gavin trotted ahead of him, displaying all the energy and resilience of youth. Mike couldn't help but look again in the direction Sarah had gone.

For whatever reason, he had to admit that there was something about her, the way she spoke or carried herself, *something* that he couldn't put his finger on that, he might as well admit, had...excited him.

He turned to the task at hand and took the shovel back from Gavin, hoping the chore would banish further thoughts along those lines.

"Go back and find something to wrap poor Devon in," he said to his son.

Gavin made a face. "Aw, no, why, me?"

"Go on, Gavin, he won't bite you." Donovan pierced the earth with the shovel and threw the load of dirt behind him. Gavin retreated to the house, muttering unhappily under his breath as he went.

Mike dug for a full five minutes without thinking, then jammed the shovel into the earth and rested his arm on the handle while he waited for Gavin to reappear. It was almost like he'd seen the episode on the porch before. Like he'd experienced it in a movie or something.

An American movie.

He glanced again in the direction she had gone.

A really interesting American movie.

IT RAINED NEARLY the whole way back to the cottage. The dark night and the rain had reduced Sarah's visibility to just a few feet in front of her but she took solace in the fact that Dan knew the way home. It was a strange feeling, she noted, with rain and darkness all around—and wickedness, too—to just let Dan carry her home without worrying about how.

As a long cold finger of rain finally found its way down her collar, she thought it just might be the first time she had ever voluntarily let someone or something else handle things. She just knew she couldn't do it all herself. It was enough to stay upright on the horse—she was so tired—without trying to figure which road to take. Her earlier plans to trot all the way back were abandoned because of the wet roads and slick trails. She let Dan pick his pace and his path.

About a quarter mile from where she estimated the cottage should be, she felt something was different about the ride. As bumpy and uneven as it had been up to now, it felt now that Dan was limping. Groaning at her bad luck, Sarah stopped him and slid to the ground. Her legs instantly gave way beneath her and she landed in a cold puddle of water in the road.

Dirty snow was piled up along the sides of the road. With shaking hands, she ran her fingers down Dan's hock and lifted his front left foot. A sharp rock the size of her thumbnail was pushing against his frog. Without a pick, and the rain sluicing down her face, she used her fingers to pry it out and tossed it away. Even so, she decided not to remount, whether because she doubted she would be able to haul herself back up into the saddle or because Dan's hoof needed the break, she wasn't sure.

She led him a hundred yards up the first rise where she saw something that made her stop and gasp. Tears sprang to her eyes.

Their cottage appeared in a ghostly shadow less than a quarter of a mile away. A thin curl of smoke came from the chimney, a welcome and a promise of warmth and love that filled her with strength and joy, and a feeling of comfort and God's presence as strong as she had ever felt before in her life.

With the rain dripping off her jacket, the mud covering the tops of her boots, she led her limping horse home.

Dear Mom and Dad,

I cannot even tell you how cold it is here! Somehow, when I thought of Ireland, I thought of the rain but I didn't think of the bone-piercing cold. I asked John if we were at the same parallel as Canada but he just gave me one of those looks he gives when he thinks I should at least try to act like the parent and know more than he does!

We've been getting along pretty good since I last wrote you. It's hard work but we're healthy, we're (relatively) warm, and we have enough to eat. I went into town yesterday to swap some nonessential things we had (wine, mostly) for some things we could really use (tools, mostly). Seems the Irish considered the wine in the "essential things" category and I did very well in my trading! I'll be hard pressed to just pay the marked prices for things when I get back to civilization. I'm really getting the hang of haggling. (Ha ha.)

Anyway, I met a young woman at the market who has a major problem and it turns out we were in a position to help her. Her husband was killed earlier in the month and she has two small children who depend on her. She seems to have enough provisions and she says her little farm is easily run by just herself (although I cannot imagine how...these people are a different breed from us, y'all. They are so tough and resourceful.)

But part of her well caved in and she can't repair it on her own. She suggested a week's worth of work from David (seems there are a few other things she needs doing while she's got an able-bodied man) and she'd give us one of her dairy cows. I know it sounds absurd, probably, from your end, but having a cow would make a BIG difference in our lives here. John needs the milk; the young woman—Julie—needs our help. So, this is a long way of saying that David left this morning for a week away from us. I can't say he was thrilled with the idea but he did reflect in an amused tone: "Who would've guessed I'd end up being more prized for my brawn than my brain?" Thought you'd get a chuckle out of that, Dad. Anyway, I'm already counting the days until he's back. As hard as it is here, it's a lot harder when fifty percent of your workforce is gone!

So I must leave you until next time. It's late and my candle is down to a nub. Take care of each other. I pray you are both well, and that, whatever happens, you won't worry about us over here. We are all fine.

Love,

Sarah

SARAH FOLDED her letter and carefully tucked it away with the rest of the unmailed letters home. The rain was tattooing out a gentle beat against the kitchen window. She wondered where David was sleeping tonight. She hoped it was better than a patch of hay in the barn at Julie's place. Sarah looked over at John, asleep in the big bed, and smiled.

Before David left, they had decided to mark out the garden for the spring planting upon his return. Dierdre had promised them cuttings and seeds and David had found more seeds in the root cellar.

Since Julie said she had several rifles and all her husband's tools, David only took a knife with him for protection on his ride to Balinagh. Sarah smiled again thinking back at the moment that John determined (incorrectly, she told herself) that that meant one of the two guns left behind was his.

She pulled her sweater tighter around her and went to check the stove. She decided they would not use the fireplace while David was gone. The little potbellied stove was more efficient for warming up the room. She opened the little stove door with an oven mitt and wedged in another couple of sticks of wood. The stove would be ice-cold when they awoke in the morning, but the mountains of blankets—and each other—would keep them snug and warm until then.

· · ·

TEN DAYS LATER, David still hadn't come back.

14

As she had every freezing cold morning since David left, Sarah left her warm bed, started the cook fire in the kitchen and went to the front door to see if she might glimpse him coming down the main drive. As if her watching for him might make him come. She knew it was possible that David just hadn't finished the work he'd agreed to do for the girl, but she couldn't imagine he wouldn't come home to tell her that. It wasn't like David to just...not return.

She turned back to the kitchen and pulled out a bowl of dough and began forming it into biscuits. She would make enough for all three of their meals today. The pan she had set on the stove was boiling so she poured the tea. A little-boy groan from the bed brought a smile to her lips.

"Morning, sweetie," she said as she mixed sugar and goat milk into a mug for him. "Sleep okay?"

John made a muffled response. She brought his tea to him and set it down on the table next to the bed.

"Dad here?" he asked sleepily.

"Not yet. I'll bet he'll get in later this afternoon."

"That's what you said yesterday."

John sat up and reached for his tea.

"Blow on it," she said. *He looked like such a little boy. Who would he be when they finally made it back home?*

Sarah went back to the kitchen and felt a weight press down on her shoulders.

Where are you, David? Your family needs you here.

She slid the biscuits in the oven and sat down at the kitchen table with her own mug of tea.

The woman she'd traded with for the six sheep had come the first day after David left and collected her sheep and the wine. She wasn't friendly and Sarah worried that she saw the woman looking around, taking inventory of the cottage and barn.

Will I ever be able to trust people again? she wondered.

Today, she and John would go round up their remaining sheep. She'd decided they needed to be able to *see* their sheep. Besides, they had lost two to the cold in just the last week. As John had reminded her: "We don't have an endless supply of sheep, you know." They would move them to the patch of grass on the other side of the paddock.

The rabbit traps had been empty for several days now and Sarah doubted they'd catch any more until spring. There was still some canned food in the root cellar, three chickens and one rooster and plenty of flour for bread. It might be a meatless winter, but at least they'd survive.

Sarah stood up and went to the front door again.

"You said probably this afternoon," John said from the bed.

"That's right. I was just looking."

John climbed out of bed. "You were watching."

"You're right," she said with a smile. "I guess I was."

IT WAS when David had been gone a total of two weeks that John began to push to go after him.

"I know the way to Balinagh," he said. "It's just straight down that road. Even *you* did it in the pouring rain and it was no big deal."

"He's not in Balinagh," she said for the hundredth time.

"It doesn't matter, Mom," John said with exasperation. "*Someone* will know where she lives. Everybody knows everyone in Ireland."

They'd had scrambled eggs for supper with toast and what was left of the jam Dierdre had given them the month before.

"He might need me," John said. "He might be hurt somewhere and needing me to come."

Sarah could feel the tears coming.

"This, I think, we have to give to God." Sarah sat down next to him and put her arms around him.

"You mean, like accept we can't do anything?"

"Well, we can pray, you know?"

John stood up. "No," he said.

"Now, John..." Sarah said.

"God helps them that helps themselves," he said stubbornly. "I think God's wondering how long it'll take before we get up and go look for him. I do, Mom."

Sarah felt a catch in her throat as she watched her boy, so resolute, so sure of himself.

"Mom?" John sat back down next to her. "You okay?"

She forced the tears back and smiled at him. "I'm fine. And you're right. We'll go first thing in the morning."

"Really?" John jumped again and clapped his hands in his excitement. "Why do we have to wait 'til morning? It's nowhere near dark yet. It'll take me two secs to saddle everybody up."

Sarah put a hand out to calm him and felt a strong rush of love and certainty, as if God Himself were blessing the enterprise.

"First thing in the morning," she said.

.   .   .

THE NEXT MORNING Sarah and John stood in the doorway of the barn with their reins in their hands and watched the rain pour down.

I hate Ireland, Sarah thought.

"We're still going, right?" John asked, looking from the rain to his mother's face as if trying to decipher her thoughts.

Sarah sighed.

"We are still going," she said. *I must be crazy.* "Put the dogs in the stall with their water bowl and mount up," she said, looping the reins over Dan's head. "Wear your hardhat, John. I don't know when you stopped wearing it but..." She didn't bother finishing. He was back in one of the stalls not listening anyway.

He rejoined her, his hardhat on and buckled, and climbed onto his pony.

"Put your shirt collar up," she said. "Or else the rain'll go straight down your back."

"Mom, I'm good," he said, moving his pony out into the rain. "Let's *go.*"

They walked at a steady, slow plod for an hour. The rain hammered them the whole way. The road had turned to slick mud and Sarah forbade John to break into a trot. She kept the gun in her unsnapped holster and let Dan find the best spots on the road to walk while she scanned the bushes and the horizon for any signs of *anything* that might want to do them harm.

Although what lunatic would be out in this weather?

She and John spoke very little. She could tell by the determined look on his face that he was thinking of his father, possibly envisioning scenarios of rescue or, at least, reunion.

Hope is a wonderful thing, she thought. Did she think they would find David?

If he was anywhere close, he wouldn't have stayed away so long. It was that simple.

She hoped to find a clue in town, or a piece of information that would lead them further down the trail. But it was beyond

even her to believe that the day would end with their arms
around their beloved one.

Even if she *hadn't* been lost in thought when the thunder
crashed down on them, she still would have lost control of Dan.

She had been riding just long enough to be confident that she
wouldn't come off him at a walk.

She was wrong.

The horse shied at the loud clap and wheeled sharply to
gallop back toward home. Sarah didn't survive the turn.

She tumbled from the saddle onto the hard, muddy road,
cracking her helmet as she hit. Somewhere in the distance she
could hear John yelling and then everything went gently black.

JULIE SLIPPED OUT of the bed, peeling the dirty sheets back and
trying to ignore if anything crawled out as she moved. She looked
over her shoulder at Mack still asleep. He normally didn't sleep.
He had come to bed late and drunk. There had been no
conversation.

How different from Arden he was, she thought before she could
stop herself.

There's no point in going down that road.

She crept out the door of the trailer. The camp was quiet.
Most of the men and the few women were still asleep under blankets and molding quilts scattered about on the ground near the
now-spent fire.

Julie tiptoed to a private spot in the woods and relieved
herself. The air was icy cold but she hadn't bothered putting her
shoes on. She looked up to inspect the sky. Dark clouds were
moving in.

Mack would be awake when she got back. It had been a rare
gift to have awakened first. She would need to hurry if she didn't
want to spend half the morning calming his anger.

When she came back to the bedroom in the trailer, he was sitting up, his arm bandage dirty and blotchy with dried blood. She couldn't remember if she'd ever seen him bathe. He was waiting for her.

"Sorry," she said, slipping back into bed, careful not to let her cold feet touch his. She'd paid the price for *that* mistake early on.

"Anybody else up yet?" he asked.

She shook her head.

"Did you make tea?" He asked it as if expecting an obvious affirmative. She cursed herself for not thinking of it. *Should she lie?*

"I put the water on," she said. "But I might've forgotten to boost up the fire." She pulled the covers back to jump up and amend the oversight when he stopped her.

"Never mind," he said. "Someone will be up soon and they'll do it."

She returned to her place in bed, watching him.

"How long would you say the Yank has been at your Mum's?" he asked.

The question surprised her. Under Mack's orders, she had lured the American to her mother's farm nearly two weeks earlier. Until this moment, Finn had not mentioned it again.

She licked her lips. "About a fortnight, I think," she said.

"And you checked on him?"

She nodded. "I went to visit me Mum yesterday," she said.

"And saw him?"

She nodded again. "He...he had had an accident."

Mack's eyes flashed to hers from the spot on the ceiling he had been studying.

"What kind of accident?"

"He...I...I think he fell," she said, hoping Mack wouldn't kill her. She had seen enough evidence of his cruelty to his men and the occasional wandering traveler to know what he was capable of.

"But he's still alive."

"Yes, yes," she said. "He's alive, but...but..."

"But what Jules?" The look he gave her was as deadly as any pit viper's. She tried to calm herself enough to answer him.

"But me Mam's got him restrained...from leaving, you see," she finished, feeling a thin residue of sweat developing on her upper lip.

Mack looked at her and then burst out laughing.

"'*Restrained* from leaving'?" he asked, still laughing. "That's beautiful." He grinned at her. "How about we visit her today? Would you like that, Jules? So we can relieve her of her responsibility."

Julie watched his gaze return to the invisible spot on the ceiling, his smile slowly fading. "Aye," he said more to himself than anyone else, "I think today's the day to be doing exactly that."

"Mom! Mom! Are you okay?"

Sarah felt the cold and the wet before she opened her eyes. It was dark out but whether that was really the case or just in her head, she couldn't tell. John was kneeling next to her, holding his pony's reins.

"Mom, you fell. Are you okay? Oh, gosh, Mom, can you please be okay?"

Hearing the panic in her son's voice, Sarah struggled to swim back to full consciousness. It was so dark.

"I'm okay, John," she said. "I'm okay."

"Oh, Mom, I was so scared. Are you sure you're okay?"

Her head hurt badly. She put a shaky hand to her face and saw John wince as she did so.

"You're bleeding, Mom. A whole bunch, like everywhere."

"Where...where's Dan?" she asked.

"He's over there. He ran for a while and then he came back.

But he's all trembling and he's limping, too. I think I saw him fall down."

Oh, God.

"Help me up, sweetie."

"Are you sure, Mom?"

"Just to sit up." Sarah had to admit, between the rain, the darkness and the blood dribbling down her face, it was difficult to see. Worse, what she *was* seeing was slightly double.

Great. A concussion.

"Is it...is it night already?" she said, looking around. She had landed squarely in the middle of the road.

"It's kind of night," John said, standing up and absently patting his pony. "Or maybe it's just the storm making it feel like night."

"How long was I out?"

"I don't know. Maybe fifteen minutes?"

"That's a long time."

"Well, maybe it wasn't that long. I'm not good at times."

"It's all right, sweetie," she said, feeling like her breakfast was about to come up. "Can you go bring Dan over here and let's check him out?"

Glad to have something specific to do, John led his pony over to where Dan was grazing in the rain. Sarah threw up onto the road.

How far are we from Balinagh? she wondered, trying to wipe her face with her jacket sleeve. She eased her helmet off. She could feel the crack in it with her fingers and wondered if wearing it broken would be any help at all. When she saw how badly Dan was limping as John led him over to her, she realized it didn't matter.

Nobody was going to be riding anywhere.

. . .

THE NIGHT WAS NEARLY UNBEARABLE. The rain never let up for a moment. It took Sarah an hour just to climb back on her feet. At some point, without her having to say the words, John realized they would not be going the rest of the way to Balinagh today. It was arguable at this point whether they were closer to home or the village.

It never occurred to Sarah when they set out to walk back home that they might not make it before morning. She underestimated how hurt she was and they had to stop frequently. She and John took turns riding Star but, even so, it was clear they were all exhausted and would do better to hole up some place for the night rather than try to forge on.

"I remember a place, maybe," John said to her when she was eyeing a ditch for their bedding down. "A kind of broken down cottage or something across the pasture a ways. I saw it when we came out this morning."

Was that really just this morning? It felt like a week since they'd set out on their journey to rescue David.

"Is it far?" Sarah's head ached fiercely and it seemed that Dan's limp was becoming more pronounced. "What if there are snakes or rats inside?"

"No snakes in Ireland," John said cheerfully. "Besides it's the wrong time of year for them. Let me ride ahead and check it out, okay? It's better than sleeping out in the open."

She couldn't argue with that and she was so tired and miserable, she honestly couldn't see how things could get much worse. She let him go.

She hadn't taken ten steps when he was back, trotting when she'd begged him to stay at a walk, and excited to lead her back to the place he'd found.

It would do.

The shed, and it wasn't much more than that, was shelter from the rain and the quickly dropping temperatures. It was open on one side, like a lean-to. They were able to hobble the horses at one end of the shed while they huddled in the other. John wanted a fire, but Sarah was afraid to allow it.

Together, the two of them endured a long wet night, punctuated once with what could only have been the sound of a gunshot. Not near, but not far enough away, either.

At one point, when Sarah thought he was asleep, John asked her: "Is this a message from God, do you think?"

Sarah couldn't help but laugh. "You mean, like maybe He wants us to leave it to Him, after all?"

"Do you think?"

"I don't know, sweetheart," she said tiredly. "Maybe He wants us to try harder. Maybe it's just bad luck and it doesn't mean anything at all."

John ruminated for a moment.

"I'd hate to think He sent a thunder clap our way," he said finally.

She kissed him on the cheek. "Try to get some sleep, sweetie."

"Mom?"

"Yes, sweetheart?"

"We'll try again to find Dad as soon as Dan is better?"

"We will. I promise. Now go to sleep."

Sarah leaned against a wooden support beam, the gun in her lap, and slept more than she stood sentry.

In the morning, both horses had hobbled out into the surrounding pasture and the rain had stopped. Her forehead was crusted with dried blood, the cut over her right eye where she had fallen, was sore but not deep. Both she and John were badly chafed from having slept in their wet clothes.

As soon as it was light enough to see one foot in front of the other, they began the long walk home.

DEAR MOM AND DAD,

Well, David's been gone for a little over a month now. John and I tried to go out and find him a couple of weeks ago but ended up with a lame horse and never made it to Ballinagh. We'll try again as soon as Dan can walk again without limping. I don't really know what happened to him but John thinks he fell. (I did, too, but I'm fine.) He probably twisted an ankle or something. He seems to be getting better, thank God. I know I couldn't shoot him if it came to that but I guess you're supposed to.

Anyway, Christmas is next week and it's really, really cold here. John and I haven't seen a soul since the people came last month to collect the sheep I'd traded them. David was the one who brought us news from Dierdre and Seamus and without him we don't even know how they're doing or what's going on. It's so cold that, mostly, John and I stay indoors even in the daytime.

We do the chores we have to do, clean out the stalls, feed all the animals, and that's about it. We moved the sheep up closer to us which isn't working out great (for them or us!) but I'm afraid if I move them back to the pasture I won't have any sheep left come spring. At the rate they're dying, even here at the farm, I may not have any left anyway.

As far as David being gone so long, I won't lie to you, I'm pretty worried. I cannot imagine what would prevent him from returning home, unless he's hurt. I'm dying for us to ride to Balinagh, find out where this Julie lives, and go bring him home. I cannot go alone on John's pony and leave John here by himself. If Dan doesn't snap out of his injury soon, we'll walk to town. We did it once before. The problem with that is that there were rumors of roving bands of thugs going around robbing travelers and the less time spent on the roads, the better

I think I know in my heart that David hasn't come home because he's being prevented somehow. I can't imagine how. And it's so hard keeping an optimistic affect with John when I really just want to scream myself.

So, take care of each other, you two. I hated missing Thanksgiving this year and now not being with you for Christmas. We'll make it up in all the wonderful holidays to come. Promise.

Love,

Sarah

P.S. We celebrated John's eleventh birthday this week. It wasn't very jolly and I had nothing but promises to give him for a gift. (Although I did give him a coupon good for one free week of no stall mucking!) When I think of all the money I spent on his birthdays in the past, from moon walks to booking entire game rooms, it's a little amazing that, aside from not having his Dad here, it wasn't too bad.

CHRISTMAS DAY MARKED six weeks plus three days that David had been gone. Sarah knew that David not getting home for Christmas was not a good sign. It meant there was now not a hint of a possibility that he wasn't somehow being prevented from coming back to them.

If he were still alive.

Sarah sometimes allowed the unthinkable to appear in her thoughts, like a dangerous enemy she was always on the look-out for.

"Pretty crappy Christmas," John said brushing the fur of the dog, Patrick, by the fireplace. The other puppy, Spongy, was curled up on the floor, his chin resting on John's knee. To mark the special day, Sarah had allowed a fire in the hearth.

"Is that my hairbrush you're using?"

John tossed the brush on the couch.

"No presents, no turkey." He paused. "No Dad."

Sarah had been sitting in the big chair by the fire, one of the two large rugs she had knitted from their sheep's wool lay across her lap. She had a steaming mug of hot tea in her hands and given all that she had lost, felt strangely content.

"A savior was still born today," she said.

He made a face.

"Well, he was born all those other Christmases, too, and it didn't stop us from having presents and stuff. I didn't think it was an either or."

Sarah smiled into her mug of tea so he wouldn't see her amusement.

"I know, John," she said. "We've got the best part of Christmas, though. That's what we need to remember."

"How can it be the best part with Dad not here?"

"We just need to have faith he'll come back to us. Today of all days, we just need to believe."

Before the words were fully out of her mouth, there was a knock at the door that made them both jump. Sarah spilled her tea and John bolted for the front door.

"John! Wait!"

But he already snatched the latches off and pulled the door open, expecting, Sarah realized later, his father to be standing there, probably with a Christmas goose in one hand and an Xbox 360 in the other.

By the time Sarah untangled herself from the heavy blanket and stumbled to the door, John was already off the porch and pulling boxes out of Dierdre's pony trap that stood directly outside the cottage.

Dierdre stood on the porch, her coat wrapped around her shoulders, a tremulous smile on her lips.

"Happy Christmas, darlin.' We brought Christmas dinner."

15

When David opened his eyes the room was so dark that at first he wasn't sure his eyes were really open. His lips were cracked and dry, his throat parched.

The last time he'd awakened...*was it really the last time?*...she had tried to help him relieve himself in a pail by the side of the bed. The ensuing mess that followed had resulted in a harsh slap to his already throbbing face and a shrill threat to withhold water in future.

A threat she had obviously made good on.

David licked his lips. How long had it been since he'd had water? How long had he been tied to this filthy bed?

As the morning light from a window filtered into the room, David's eyes filled with tears at the prospect of another day.

Dear God, will I ever see Sarah and John again? Are they okay?

How long had he been gone? Had they come looking for him? A tremor of fear coursed through him. If they made it as far as the old woman's farm, they would either be turned away or killed. And he had no way of knowing which.

The woman, Betta, told him daily that no one was looking for him. Once, she told him she heard that the two Americans had left to go to Dublin. As desperately alone and abandoned as that news made him feel, a part of him prayed it was true. There was no way Sarah could survive and take care of John out here. At least in the city there might be provisions for refugees. He cursed himself for allowing them to stay.

What had he been thinking? That they could hold out in the midst of Mad Max 2.0 and survive?

Recently the woman had begun talking about a gang of gypsies that was going from village to village, murdering whole families, taking food, slaughtering the livestock. She was terrified they were coming for her next. She talked incessantly of how she might secure the farm against them. She begged for his advice, promising to free him so he could protect them both.

Yesterday, she told him the American woman and her son hadn't left after all. She said she heard that the gypsies had murdered them. She had wept for his loss.

His stomach muscles tensed as he heard her beginning to move about in the other end of the farmhouse. This signaled the fact that his nightmare would resume shortly.

He had ridden to Balinagh, however many weeks or months ago now he couldn't tell, and met Julie. She was waiting for him in front of where Siobhan's store used to be. She sat on a small Highland pony, her hair down to her waist, looking like something in an Irish fairytale.

Why hadn't he taken one look at the pretty lassie in her pastel gypsy dancing skirt and realized what a lie she must be? Did he even question it? Did he even wonder, if she really was a widow with two small children and a farm to run, who was at home taking care of everything while she was perched on a pony, her hair flowing in the wind?

No, he saw what he wanted to see. A damsel in distress. Not what she really was—bait for a trap.

David struggled to a sitting position. The light was strong enough now for him to take inventory of the room and of himself.

The room was small, just big enough for the single bed he lay on and a dresser filled, he knew, with the old woman's dead husband's clothes. His left arm, broken in two places, was strapped to his chest.

It had stopped hurting him weeks ago, whether because it had finally mended or died itself he had no way of knowing. Both legs were loosely tied to the end of the bed. His right arm was manacled to a long chain attached to a boat anchor, rusting in the corner of the room.

When he'd first arrived at the farm with Julie, he immediately saw the disrepair of the place. But there were no cows that he could see and no children. Julie took him into the farmhouse where a woman in her late fifties sat at the table. She broke into a broad grin, her teeth yellowed and brown, and clapped her hands in delight.

PAINFULLY, he remembered that afternoon.

"Saints be praised, you've come," the woman at the table said.

"I'm glad to help, ma'am," he said. "You are Julie's mother?"

"Sure, can't you tell?" The woman laughed but Julie did not join in.

"Please sit and have a cuppa, you'll be tired from your ride in from town."

David sat down in one of the kitchen chairs.

"I didn't realize your place was so far from Balinagh. It took us nearly four hours to ride here."

"Sure, it's a great long way," the woman said. "Which is why the needing of a man was so desperate."

David looked at Julie. "So it's not you who needs help? It's your mother?"

Julie looked away and her mother answered for her.

"Sure, nobody would come help an ugly crow like me," she

said laughing. "You'll not be blaming Julie for our little ruse, eh? I practically had to beat her to do it."

Julie looked at David.

"I'm sorry, mister," she said. "But me mum needs help, same as you thought I did. No difference."

Except for the part about being lied to, David thought with growing anger. But he said: "You're right. And I'm here now." He stood up. "Can you show me the well?" He looked at the older woman. "Was that part true? You have a well that's collapsed?"

"Ah, sure, don't be mad at us, now," The woman said. "Plenty of time for that and too late to get started today, so it is. I'm called Betta, by the by. And yourself?"

IT DIDN'T MATTER how many times he'd told her what his name was. She always called him Danny. He'd been on the farm a total of two days when he fell off a ladder, hit his head and broke his arm. Julie had left long since.

At first, Betta had been the soul of care while he lay helpless. The head injury was the most disabling, preventing him from getting out of bed for days. During that time, Betta fed him, cleaned him, and sang to him as he dipped in and out of consciousness.

She set the broken bone, badly, but in the way of country-women who have had to do this and worse many times over the years—efficiently if painfully. Gradually, David got stronger. His head cleared and he spent more and more time out of bed, even if it was just to shuffle to the outhouse and back.

The stronger he got, the more anxious Betta seemed to become.

One morning, he awoke to discover she'd crept into his room and chained him to the boat anchor. He could move about the room but not leave it. When he broke the bed and the window frame in an attempt to free himself, she waited again until he'd fallen into an exhausted sleep, slipped in and tied his feet to the bed.

That had been weeks ago.

David developed pressure ulcers lacerating his backside and thighs and he could feel the muscles in his legs shorten by the day. His hours consisted of threatening her and begging her to free him.

She begged him to agree to stay willingly. She said she wanted to trust him. She wanted to let him go. There was much work to do on the place.

Once, she got close enough and he was able to grab her by the throat with his weak arm. He could've killed her, but in the end he couldn't do it. The next day she drugged his food and strapped his good arm to his chest. He remembered feeling relief she hadn't broken it.

SARAH WORKED the knots out of the small of her back with her fingers. Dierdre snored loudly on the couch, bundled up in two wool rugs and one of John's dogs. The fire was long gone cold.

Her arrival last night had been their Christmas miracle. Just the motions of welcoming someone to their hearth on such a special night reminded Sarah of Christmases past. And Dierdre had brought dinner. A roast chicken with potatoes and even gravy. A veritable feast.

Sarah walked to the stove to light it. She took a moment to warm her hands around the flame and then closed the oven door and began pulling cold biscuits from the breadbox.

What Dierdre had *not* brought with her was Seamus.

Sarah eyed the grey clouds from her kitchen window. It was cold but it didn't look like more snow on the way. She put a pan of water on the hot stove.

As if I'd know snow clouds from any other kind, she thought to herself. And then she stopped. The fact was, after weeks of observing them, she *did* know which clouds spelled snow and which ones didn't. The thought surprised her.

But snow or not, she would need to leave their snug little cottage today. Now that Dierdre was here to stay with John, Sarah could finally go to Balinagh and see if there was any word on David. In fact, that was the first thought out of John's mouth when he realized that Dierdre had come to stay. He'd blurted it out over dinner and his words brought tears to Dierdre's eyes.

"Sure, I knew there must be a reason why we hadn't seen your David in so long," Dierdre said. "I told Seamus something awful bad must've happened." Dierdre looked meaningfully at Sarah and Sarah knew it was because she needed her to go back to the farm and find Seamus, too.

He'd walked off two days earlier. Given the weather, Dierdre wasn't optimistic, but neither could she rest until he was found.

"But, there's no hope for Seamus," John had blurted out, looking from Sarah to Dierdre. "*Dad* might still be alive."

"Of course, of course," Dierdre patted his hand. "Your mother must go and find your da. Seamus can wait, sure he can." But her eyes were sorrowful and belied her words.

Sarah poured the tea and mixed milk and sugar into two mugs. John would sleep a little longer but she could see that Dierdre was awake now. She realized how good it felt to have an extra person in the cottage. Dierdre was a strong countrywoman and a font of useful information and skills. Having her stay with them would make everything so much easier.

"Sure, you don't have to be waitin' on me, darlin'," Dierdre said as she shuffled into the kitchen.

"I don't mind," Sarah said, handing the woman her tea.

"Needing to feel useful, are ye?" Dierdre laughed and sat in one of the kitchen chairs.

"I probably will never need to 'feel useful' again in my whole life," Sarah admitted. "I've never felt more essential and at the same time more irrelevant to our survival than I do here."

"As soon as life gets too much for us, we finally let go and allow the Almighty his turn."

"I guess it takes a world crisis to make us realize we're not in control."

"Nor were we ever."

Sarah placed the toasted biscuits on a plate with a dish of jam and goat butter between them. She sat down and cupped her own mug of tea.

"I'll go find Seamus today," she said.

Dierdre looked at her over her mug. "And then you intend to go on to Balinagh afterwards." It wasn't a question.

Sarah looked outside the kitchen window. "I can do both."

"Sure, the needin' to know is a powerful thing," Dierdre said, watching her. "I'll not talk you out of it. I know he's gone, my Seamus." She put her mug down and stared out the window. "It's just that..."

"I know." Sarah touched the old woman's hand.

"I wish you could've know him," Dierdre said. She shook her head. "Sure, I see what you see...an addled old man who can't remember his way home from the woodshed, but my God he was a force in his day, so he was."

"Mike Donovan said he was the village school teacher."

"Well, that's true but I'll be surprised if that's what people remember Seamus for."

"What do you mean?"

Dierdre took a deep breath and Sarah could see she was fighting her emotions.

"Seamus was the handsomest lad in the village, years ago. The glint in his eye was matched by the brightness of his wit. Oh, he had a tongue. Every lass in Balinagh was in love with him, so they were."

"But you got him," Sarah said, her eyes moving to John's form in bed wondering if he were asleep or listening.

"If you could've known him," Dierdre said. "As alive and bright as any could be...that he chose me was mystery enough. To end up...to end up..."

Sarah touched her hand again. "I'll find him, Dierdre. I promise I'll find him."

Dierdre nodded, her tears falling now. "Please, God," she said.

BETTA STOOD by David's bed and wrung her hands. Her face was florid as if she'd just run a race, her hands were grey with grime. She was looking at him as if she expected him to levitate or spontaneously combust at the very least.

David's stomach growled. He couldn't remember the last time she had brought food to him. His head was aching. It was all he could do to speak.

"I need water, Betta," he said, hearing his voice sounding more like a croak. "I can't help you unless you give me water."

Betta appeared not to hear him.

"What could I do?" she said to him. "I did what I thought was best. Did I do right, Danny? Did I?"

David tried to wrap his mind around what she was saying but she been nonsensically ranting for weeks now and the effort to understand her usually mattered little in the end. He closed his eyes.

"You did right," he whispered. "Water, Betta. Please, water."

She pulled up a chair to the bed.

"Margie and Jamie came this morning, did you know? Did you hear? Sure, you must've heard them."

David tried to remember who they were. His brain seemed to have stopped working. He licked his dry lips.

"You heard them, Danny, didn't you? Didn't you?"

David opened his eyes. "They were...people were...here?" he managed.

"Margie and Jamie, I told you," she said with impatience. "They just left. I know you saw them." She stood up and jerked open the curtain across the window in the room which looked out over the entrance to the house. "You saw them and you heard me tell them I was alone here." She sounded like she had caught him in a terrible crime.

"My...my horse..." He stuttered as he realized rescue had been minutes from his front door and he had slept through it.

"Your horse is in the barn. I'm telling you they believed me when I told them I was alone."

A single tear escaped his eye and found its way down his face.

"You hate me, don't you?" she said. Her voice was flat. "You hate me for keeping you here."

David looked at her face. Through the haze of hunger and blighted memory, he could see her insanity. His words formed slowly as if he were speaking through cotton.

"Don't hate you," he said, closing his eyes again as exhaustion and sickness carried him back to unconsciousness.

"Forgive you," he said.

16

Sarah stood in the barn brushing Dan. The physical exertion helped the roiling anxiety in her stomach. He was so big she had to stretch to brush his back and when she'd finished her shoulders ached.

The disappointment of having to push her expedition back was intense. The rain had started right after breakfast and turned into snow soon after.

So much for being able to tell anything from the clouds, she thought.

As Dierde said—as bitterly disappointed as the old woman was—there was no sense going and ending up frozen and lost herself.

No one was more disappointed than John. Two people they all loved were somewhere out in that swirling maelstrom of white and cold, two people who needed their help and who would have to wait a little longer.

No one needed to say out loud that the longer wait could be the death of both.

Sarah cleaned Dan's feet and ran her hands each of his legs. He nickered and turned to look at her. She put her arms around his neck and buried her face in his mane, just like she used to do when she was a horse-crazy teenager with a problem that only her pony could understand.

Could David really be still alive? Was he out there somewhere trying to get back to us?

The agony of not knowing coiled in her stomach like a black knot.

Was this really how it would end for him? A brilliant accountant, loved by his colleagues and clients, admired and respected. Was this really how it was to end for him? Riding off into the Irish countryside never to be seen again?

Sarah laced her fingers in Dan's mane. The big horse shifted his weight but otherwise stood quietly. Over his shoulder through the plastic of the barn window, she watched the snow fall.

God help me, she thought. *Will I not even be able to go tomorrow?*

THE SOUNDS CAME to David as if they were part of the feverish dream he was having. At first, he couldn't be sure what was real. But as the voices got louder, he found himself being jolted awake. His bedroom was dim but his view of the front of the house was unobstructed by the curtains Betta had pulled back earlier that day.

The loud voices came from the front of the house. He could hear men. Underneath it all, he heard the terror in Betta's high falsetto voice.

She was pleading. He had heard that begging shrill voice even in his nightmares. Outside, he glimpsed a crowd of people in the front yard. They were trampling Betta's garden.

He heard three gunshots, one right after another. Betta's horrible wailing scream grew higher and higher.

David struggled to sit up and pulled uselessly against his

restraints. His legs were covered in bedsores that wept onto the dirty linens. His left arm lay impotently against his chest, duct-taped around his upper body. He pulled against the chain attached to the boat anchor with his free hand.

He saw one of the men drag Betta down into the front garden. His hand moved in a jerking motion and Betta sagged to her knees into the dahlias, blood spurting from her throat.

David jerked up and rasped out the single word "No!" It felt like barely more than a whisper, but the killer, wiping his blade on his shirt, turned and looked directly at David through the open window.

DIERDRE MADE DINNER THAT NIGHT. Sarah couldn't remember being more moved by such a simple act. To have any responsibility at all taken from her shoulders was an incredible gift. John was quiet. He sat between his two dogs, absentmindedly petting them both at the same time. He watched the flames in the fireplace.

"Sure, don't worry about him, Sarah," Dierdre said, nodding toward John. "The smart ones need time to think it all through. Seamus was the same way and I'll bet your David is, too."

"It's just that he's so young to have so much bad stuff to think about," she said as she watched John.

"Well, there's little you can be doing about *that*," Dierdre said. "Life is what it is. You'll not be changing it just because you don't want it troubling him."

Sarah nearly laughed. "It's weird, Dierdre. Because back home, that's exactly what I tried to do. All the time. And most of the time? I felt like I *did* change it."

Dierdre smiled. "That would be because you're American, and all. Now, no offense, but the rest of us don't have the luxury for such nonsense."

"Or the arrogance?"

"Some things are best left unsaid. Come, laddie. Here's your dinner."

John came to the table and sat down.

"Isn't it great, having Dierdre here?" Sarah said.

John looked up at her from his hands and gave her an indicting look.

"Look, sweetie, I have no control over the weather."

"I know."

Dierdre spooned up chicken casserole onto three plates.

"And we'll not want to be losing your mum out there in all this, would we?"

"I *saw* the wisdom in you not going, Mom," John muttered.

"Look, I'm not patronizing you, sweetie," Sarah said, putting her hand on his cheek. "I know you're not blaming me for the weather. And I'm disappointed, too."

His eyes filled with tears. "It's just, I keep seeing Dad in trouble and I can't help but think every minute counts. That's all."

"I know. Me, too."

Dierdre sat down at the table and reached for their hands.

"We'll be saying grace now," she said. "And with thanking the good Lord for this meal—which so many in Ireland do not have tonight—we'll also be asking Him to keep our men safe and well until they can return to us."

John looked at her and nodded. "Amen," he said. "Thanks."

THE GYPSY STRODE into the bedroom and threw back the door where it crashed into the wall with a bang. David felt like he was an actor in a B movie. An actor with no lines and no future.

"Cor! Smells like something died in here." The big gypsy stood at the end of the bed eyeing David. He was joined by two other men.

"Jaysus, Davey. She's got him chained to a boat anchor. Blimey. And us with no workin' cellphone cameras. God, but it stinks in here."

David watched the three men observe him and felt, strangely, no fear. In fact, he was surprised to note that he felt nearly joyful. The realization had just come to him that one way or the other, these men would be the method of his release from hell.

One way or the other.

"Who is he?"

"Oy! Can you speak? He's daft as a loon. Look at his eyes. Should we tell Mack?"

The gypsy, Davey, wrinkled his nose at the smell and turned on his heel to exit the room.

"Don't bother him with this shite," he said. "See if there's anything worth taking. Then kill 'im."

17

Dierdre hooked the pony to the harness. Sarah watched how quickly the older woman buckled and arranged chains along the pony's neck and back. She noticed John was watching closely too. She had no doubt he'd be able to do it himself the next time they needed to harness up the pony trap.

"Little Ned will see you fine, please God," Dierdre said, patting the pony on the neck.

They had debated whether or not Sarah should ride Dan or take the cart. But the lure of goods that Dierdre had left behind at her farm had settled the question. Sarah would go there first, look for Seamus, then load up the trap with anything she could carry from the house. Then she'd go on to Balinagh to ask for word about David.

That was the plan.

Sarah tugged on Dierdre's driving gloves and looked back at the cottage.

"You're going to be okay here?"

Dierdre handed her the driving reins.

"For the hundredth time, Sarah," Dierdre said. "We'll be fine, won't we, boyo?"

John came over and gave his mother a hug.

"We're armed, Mom," he said. "No one's messing with us."

"Yeah, about that," Sarah looked at Dierdre who shook her head.

"Stop worrying, Sarah," she said. "We will be fine. It's you that's going out in the world and you'll be needing to keep a watch out. That group of gypsies travels by day. Mind you see them before they see you."

"God, I can't believe any of this," Sarah said as she hopped up into the cart seat. "I'll be back by nightfall. Guaranteed. Okay?"

"See that you do," Dierdre said, her mouth in a firm line that made Sarah think she was trying not to cry.

"I'll find out where our men are, Dierdre." She looked at John. "I will."

"I know, Mom. Be careful is all. Be real careful."

She smiled reassuringly at him and urged the pony into a walk.

THE SNOW WAS STILL FALLING when Sarah left the cottage but she was determined to go on even if she spotted a funnel cloud hovering over the Irish dry stonewalls that lined the horizon.

Do the Irish get tornadoes? she wondered.

She had never driven a horse-drawn wagon before and it felt awkward trying to control the pony without the use of her legs or seat. She consciously worked to tamp down her anxiety and impatience but, even so, found herself urging the little pony into a trot. She prayed he could manage any slick spots on the icy road.

A video of the cart overturned and the horse hopelessly entangled in its harness and cart brackets flashed into her mind. Almost angrily, she banished the image and forced herself to slow him down to a brisk walk. She focused on the road between his ears. She remembered she used to recite poetry, or sometimes even sing, when she rode her horse years ago—after she lost her confidence and needed to rely on such techniques to calm herself and her mount.

"Dear Lord," she said outloud. "Please let me find Seamus. Dead or alive, although please alive, but in any case please let me find him so I can help Dierdre say her goodbyes." She watched the pony's ears flick backwards to catch the sound of her voice.

"And please let me find David, I beg you. I hate to ask for so much, because I need you to protect John, too, and keep him safe. And me on my trip today. Please let us get where we're going safely. Dear God, I pray."

Sarah shivered in her Gor-Tex coat and tightened her grip on the reins. When she pulled up in front of Dierdre and Seamus's little farmhouse, she was surprised to have arrived so quickly. Her thoughts had been calm and her mind open and hopeful along the way.

It occurred to her as she looked at their house that the driveway leading to it was virtually hidden from the main road. The house itself was tucked into a copse of fir trees, furthering camouflaging it. *If you didn't know it was there,* Sarah found herself thinking, *you might never find it.*

She stopped the cart, set the brake, and looked around for any sign of life. *Déjà vu,* she thought sadly, thinking of Devon. Her shoulder holster—moldy and already worn thin when she got it —now wouldn't snap shut, and she was worried the Glock, which wasn't the right size for it anyway, would fall out. She picked up the gun from the leather seat next to her and stuffed it in her jacket pocket, praying it was true what John had told her about not needing a safety on it. She jumped down from the cart.

∾

FINN SAT in Betta's kitchen drinking a mug of tea. He watched his men from the kitchen window as they fed and watered their horses. They had found several rifles in Julie's mother's house, some ammo, enough food to last them a few days, and two good horses. He recognized the Yank's big bay as one of the horses he had tried to steal two months ago when the bitch shot him.

The horse was his now, he thought with satisfaction.

A young gypsy boy entered the kitchen. His eyes were badly crossed, his skin mottled with acne. Mack marveled that the lad could take two steps without falling or crashing into something.

"Oy, Mack," the boy said. "What do you want we should do with the body?"

"What do we usually do, ye daft ejit?"

The boy looked around the room.

"Well, the rushes are set," he said.

"Mind if I finish me tea, first?"

The boy nodded and left the room.

Finn looked in the direction of the bedroom. His arm hurt him today. It didn't always. The bullet was still in there but it didn't worry him. *Didn't he have an uncle lived to seventy years with two bullets in 'im? One in each of his legs.*

Mack stood, tossed his tea mug in the sink, and walked out onto the porch. His men turned and looked at him as if awaiting orders.

"Light 'er up," he said, mounting the large, saddled, bay and turning its head toward the road. He knew he'd get a better view of the fire from the rise at the turn of the road. It was nearly his favorite part.

Nearly.

SARAH FOUND Seamus in the back bedroom.

Alive.

When she first pushed open the bedroom door and saw him,

her heart flew into her mouth and she thought, instantly, of the joy she would be bringing Dierdre who had not had the heart to hope for so much. The second thought she had, as she approached the bed where the old man lay, was that she would have to delay her trip to Balinagh and her search for David *again*.

He was awake, sitting up in bed, with a book in his hands. He watched her come without fear or recognition.

"Hey, Seamus," she said. "Am I glad to see you. Dierdre will be, too."

"Ahhh, shite, an American," he said, putting the book down.

His response startled Sarah who had not ever heard him string together enough words to form a sentence before.

"You...you remember me?"

"I went for a wee walk," he said, tiredly. "And when I returned, the wife was gone and so, of course, was any hope of lunch."

Sarah sat down on the bed next to him.

Did he have moments of clarity? Dierdre never mentioned it if he did. Sarah reached for his hand.

"Dierdre's at our place, Seamus. Let's go see her, okay? She'll have lunch ready for us."

"You're American," he said again, studying her face.

"I am," she said. "My husband and son and I are renting the McKinney place." She cleared her throat. "We're on vacation here in Ireland." The words felt absurd coming out of her mouth but she forced a smile to accompany them.

"The McKinneys," he said, frowning. "Liam McKinney is an idiot. I taught him for six years, you know." He looked out the window. "Did well in London, I'm told. Bugger me. I never would've predicted it."

Sarah stood up.

She didn't know how long this new Seamus would last but in case this was a one-off, she really wanted to get him to Dierdre as soon as possible.

"What do you want to bring with you, Seamus?" she asked

looking around the room. "Can you get yourself up while I look for a few things in the kitchen? Dierdre asked me to bring her pie pan especially."

"Yes, yes," he said, swinging his legs off the bed. He stopped and looked up at her: "Who are ye again?"

THIRTY MINUTES LATER, Sarah had the pony trap packed and the cow tethered to a lead off the back. Seamus, although dressed, was still pottering about the house and Sarah began to feel anxious to be gone and on their way back to Dierdre and John. Although the thought crossed her mind that she could still make it to Balinagh today after she dropped Seamus off—on horseback this time—she knew that the fading light and quickly dropping temperatures made the idea a bad one.

She waited by Little Ned's head, holding him by his cavesson and willing herself to be patient—even got a comical memory of herself waiting for David in their SUV while he did one last pass on checking the house—until she finally let her frustration get the better of her. She pulled the handgun out of her pocket, tossed it on the floor of the cart, and bounded up the porch steps.

"Come on, Seamus. Let's go. Lunch is on the table only it's not *this* table."

He walked toward her uncertainly, his gaze foggy and unsure.

"I've already put your bag in the cart," she said, trying to make her voice sound reassuring and cheerful. A part of her wanted to grab him and physically propel him down the steps to the cart.

"Dierdre?"

"...is waiting for you at my place, remember? Have you got everything?" She touched his elbow and he moved toward the porch.

Chatting and smiling and gently nudging, Sarah got him off the porch and into the cart. She ran around the other side of it, jumped in and collected the reins.

"Off we go," she said. *Finally.*

"Wait! Wait," Seamus said, grabbing the side of the cart.

"What is it? Can we talk about it on the road?"

"I left me glasses." He touched his breast pocket where he'd tucked a slim book of poetry. "I can't read without me glasses."

This new clear-headed *reading* Seamus was kind of a pain in the ass, Sarah found herself thinking as she laid the reins back down.

"Right, yes, okay," she said. "Where did you have them? In your bedroom?" She was already out of the cart and back up the porch steps, not waiting for an answer.

While she figured it was likely he'd go back to being catatonic before they even arrived at the cottage today, on the slim possibility he did remain clear headed, she didn't want to be the reason he spent the entire winter not being able to read. She ran to the bedroom and jerked open the nightstand. Nothing. She looked on the dresser top, then on the floor in case they'd accidentally fallen during his attempts to pack his bag.

In exasperation, she was on her hands and knees looking under the bed, pushing past dust bunnies and old books, when she heard the sound of the gunshot.

Sarah froze.

It had come from the front of the house. Where the cart was parked.

Oh, crap. Had Seamus found the gun? Her first instinct was to rush out onto the porch. Instead, she stood up, held her breath, and listened. If he'd shot himself, fifteen seconds more would not make the difference in the outcome of whatever makeshift first-aid Sarah would be able to offer him.

Voices.

She heard voices coming from outside. Silently, she moved to the bedroom wall away from the window. Dierdre and Seamus's bedroom faced the garden with a view of the well and the back pasture, but she'd left the front door open in her hurry and the voices carried easily to her.

There were at least two, maybe more, male voices. Her hand went to her jacket pocket but she knew, before she even felt inside, that the gun wasn't there.

She took a breath and edged herself across the room to catch a glimpse of what was going on outside the front door. The last time she heard voices outside a cottage door, they had been friendly ones. Just because she was terrified didn't mean these men were necessarily a threat to her.

The first thing she saw was the absence of something that should have been there but wasn't. The cow, tied to the back of the cart, sagged against the cart in a brown mountainous carcass. The results of the gunshot, she thought, her stomach roiling.

Not friends.

She pressed herself against the bedroom wall and tried to think what to do. She looked around the room for a weapon. The voices were louder now.

"Oy! We know you're in there. Come out or we shoot the auld man."

Sarah saw a shadow cross the back window. She crouched down and duck- walked out of the room just as a man stuck his head in the bedroom window. She crawled into the kitchen and wrenched a drawer open. Dierdre had already taken most of the knives and what she hadn't packed last week, were now sitting on the pony cart outside.

"She's inside!" the voice called from the back of the house. "I just saw her." The sounds of splintering wood indicated that the man was not bothering to walk around to the front to gain entrance.

Sarah grabbed the only thing she could find—a small rolling pin—and scrambled up onto the kitchen counter by the bedroom door.

"Behind you, Sean!" A voice from outside screamed. "She's behind you!"

Too late for Sean, he turned toward her as he entered the kitchen and caught the force of the rolling pin full in the face. He screamed but wrenched the rolling pin away from her as Sarah vaulted across the counter for the living room. She didn't know if there was any kind of a weapon there but all other avenues were blocked. As she ran, she heard the sound of another gunshot and this time she felt a sudden and final pressure between her shoulder blades that knocked the wind out of her.

She lay, gasping, on Dierde's living room rug, all audio turned off and the world reduced to a swirling maelstrom of color and motion.

18

They were arguing.

Three men, all of them talking at once. Sarah felt herself slide in and out of consciousness as she listened to the harsh voices. She was tied up and lying in the back of the pony cart. They had thrown most of the cart contents she had packed into the dirt. Seamus sat in front where she'd left him. The men had obviously assessed, correctly, that he posed no threat to them.

"Finn wants her alive, I tell you."

"How do you even know she's the one?"

"She's American, ye daft bugger. How many Yanks you think there are out here?" That brought about some sniggering. Sarah licked her lips. Her face felt bruised and swollen; her shoulder felt broken. The fact that they'd tied her up made her believe—made her hope—she hadn't been shot.

"Oy, she's awake."

One of the men approached the cart. He was large and pale, as if he had never seen the sun. Sarah couldn't see clearly but he appeared rough and menacing. He had a sharp ferret-face, and his small beady eyes darted around in his head as if he wasn't quite in control of them.

He jerked her to a sitting position. The pain that shot through her was like none she'd ever imagined before. She groaned.

Another man spoke from behind her. "I tell you, she's the American," he said.

The man with his hand on her raised his fist and held it to her face.

"Say something, ye stupid cow," he snarled.

Sarah looked at him blankly. He shook his fist.

"I said—"

"Go to hell," she said.

He dropped his fist. The other two laughed.

"I told ye," the one man said.

"Why does he want her?" He was watching Sarah now with curiosity. "She's not young."

"She's the one *shot* him, ye ejeet. Didn't you know?"

"Bugger me." The lout looked at Sarah with naked admiration. "And killed Ardan."

"Well, whatever he wants with her, he wants her alive. At least at first," the other man said. "Okay, Granddad, here's where you get out. Out you go, now."

Sarah directed her attention back to Seamus who was sitting quietly as if engaged in his own thoughts. He didn't move.

"Just kill 'im," the lout said, as he moved back to his horse. He pulled out a shotgun.

"It's easier if they go into the house on their own," the other man whined, "*before* we fire it. He looks heavy. I don't want to have to drag—" Even when Sarah saw Seamus reach down to the floorboards of the cart, even *she* didn't connect that he was doing anything more than scratching his ankle, so long had she considered him a nonentity.

So when he straightened in his seat and shot the young man speaking, and then turned without waiting for the body to hit the ground and shot the man pulling out the shotgun, she watched in shock.

He shot the third one in the back as he attempted to flee. Seamus never moved from his seat in the cart. When the sounds of the gunshots stopped ringing in her ears, Seamus turned to her and smiled tiredly.

"Did you happen to find my reading glasses?" he asked.

LATER THAT DAY, Sarah watched John's eyes go from hers to the window and back to hers again. In a split second he had silently asked and answered his own question. It was too late to ride to Balinagh today. She hated to disappoint him. She'd already dealt with her own letdown on the long cold ride back and had rallied herself enough to focus on the joy she was bringing to dear Dierdre.

The old woman had not wanted to untangle herself from Seamus from the moment they'd driven into the front drive of the cottage. Sarah held off revealing any details of what had happened at Dierdre's farm. When Dierdre asked why they didn't bring the cow, Sarah said only that there'd been an accident and the cow was dead. If Dierdre was disappointed about it—and surely she must have been—that emotion had no room in her heart at the moment. So joyous was she to have Seamus alive— and clear-headed—that she sat next to him, holding his hand like an awestruck schoolgirl.

It was too late for lunch by the time they had arrived back that day, but dinner was hot and filling. Dierde had roasted another chicken in anticipation of Sarah's homecoming and served it with mashed potatoes and canned creamed corn.

First thing tomorrow, Sarah mouthed the words to John. He nodded, resigned. She was tired, bone tired, and her back ached from where the big gypsy had thrown the rolling pin at her in the house. But nothing was broken. Now that she knew the face of what her fear looked like, she also knew the immensity of the task ahead of her.

She glanced at John and her heart hardened at the thought of someone trying to hurt him. Always before, when she thought of losing him she was filled with anxiety and fear. Tonight, the thought of someone taking him from her made her feel as cold and strong as granite.

A granite that could crush and kill.

Sarah looked at her glass of red wine, one of the few bottles she and David had held back from all the trading. Tonight was for celebration, she thought. It's for miracles, for loved ones raised from the dead. And for thanksgiving. She listened to Dierdre's happy, girlish prattle and let it wash over her like a job well done.

One down, she thought, taking a swallow of the dry red wine and looking at the front door with determination. *One to go.*

LATER THAT EVENING, as Sarah and Dierdre were cleaning up the dishes in the kitchen and Seamus and John sat in front of the fire, Sarah told Dierdre what had happened at the farmhouse. The old woman sucked in a sharp breath as she listened and seemed to use the table to steady herself.

"We left the cow in the drive," Sarah said quietly as she dried a plate and glanced into the living room to see if John could hear her. "The horses I untacked, stashed their saddles and bridles in the barn, and turned them out into your cow pasture."

"Dear God in heaven," the older woman murmured.

"You okay, Dierdre?" Sarah put out a hand to touch her on the shoulder. "It had to be done. It's thanks to Seamus and God Himself that it *was* done and we're here safe. You know that, right?"

"Of course, I know that," Dierdre said. "It's just..." she picked up a mug and then set it back down as if not trusting she wouldn't drop it.

"I know, I know," Sarah said, trying to whisper. "It was awful, *they* were awful. They clearly had some plan that they were going to burn the house with...with Seamus in it, like they'd done that sort of thing before."

"And sure, didn't you know?" Dierdre looked at her sharply. "Haven't you heard that there's a gang of hooligans rampaging the countryside killing and burning everything in its path?"

"Mom? You guys okay?"

"Yep, doing good," Sarah called, giving Dierdre a meaningful look. "'Bout time for you to brush your teeth, sweetheart?" She heard him speak to Seamus: "I knew I shouldn't have said anything. Now I have to go to bed."

"It's late, John," Sarah said. "Plenty of time to talk with Mr. McClenny tomorrow."

"We'll just say goodnight to the horses," Seamus called to them.

"Oh, thank you, Seamus." Sarah turned back to Dierdre. "Aren't you surprised? About Seamus?"

"You mean, him not acting daft and all?" Dierdre smiled. "It happens now and again, not for a long time now and sure, it's wonderful to have him back—in every sense of the word."

"So...it won't last? Him being lucid like this?"

"Sure, no," Dierdre said wiping down the table. "Any time now, he'll leave us again. We don't know what brings it on or why it goes away."

"Just grateful for when it comes."

"Aye," the older woman smiled and then her smile faded. "There's something else, then, isn't there, Sarah? Something you're not tellin' me."

Sarah stole a look out the window to see the two shapes of John and Seamus in front of the barn.

"There is something," Sarah admitted. She sat down at the kitchen table.

"What is it, dear? What happened?"

Sarah took a long breath and felt the agony of the day wash over her in a shroud of exhaustion and, for a moment, futility.

"It had to do with the gypsies' horses."

"The ones you turned out into the pasture? Sure, they'll be fine there until we can collect them, darlin', you'll not be worried about that."

"It's not that," Sarah said, so tired she wanted to put her head down on her arms. "One of the horses..." She turned her head as she heard Seamus and John walk across the yard toward the porch. She looked at Dierdre.

"One of the horses was Rocky," she said. "David's horse."

AFTER JOHN HAD FALLEN ASLEEP, she warned Dierdre that the gypsy she had wounded seemed intent on revenge on her.

"It makes my place a little less of a refuge for you," Sarah said.

"Nonsense," Dierdre snorted. "All it makes is you needin' us here all the more."

Even so, the next day—even before it was light—they fortified the cottage the best they could and placed loaded guns by each of the windows.

When Sarah hesitated about leaving, she only needed to see John's face to reinvigorate her conviction that she must try to find David.

She tacked up Dan, then hugged her son tightly and whispered into his ear. "Stay safe, sweetie," she said. "God willing, Dad and I will be back tonight. Just do whatever Mr. and Mrs. McClenny tell you to do, okay? If they tell you to hide, you hide. Promise me."

"I will, Mom, I promise."

Sarah rode out into the darkness, her saddlebags bulging

with cartridges, her Glock, fully loaded, in her shoulder holster. The weather was cold but clear. It hadn't snowed all night.

Again, Sarah fought the impulse to gallop Dan across the pasture in a more direct route to town. But there were too many things to make him come up lame so she held herself back. As she rode, she scanned the ditches on either side of the road for ambushes. Her fingers touched the butt of her handgun nearly the whole ride into town.

She found herself wondering when it was she had stopped being afraid of guns and when she had begun thinking of them as something comforting.

"DA, sure isn't that the American lady coming in to town?"

Mike Donovan looked up from the cart he was packing with firewood and squinted down the main street of town. It was midmorning and the sky had darkened and let loose with a gentle, insistent rain. He saw Sarah Woodson riding down the street on a large thoroughbred cross. *Most sane people would not choose to be out in this weather,* he thought.

"You're right," he said, watching her. "Wonder what she's doing here."

The town was more alive today than it had a right to be. When he and Gavin arrived earlier that morning, it was clear that a tentful of riffraff had spent the night in town drinking and fighting.

Father and son had steered wide of the noise and the crowd. Donovan needed the firewood that Siobhan kept behind her store. She was long gone and everyone else seemed to have forgotten it was even there.

The crowd of men looked to be mostly gypsies although some had a different look to them, hardened but in a city sort of way. Even from a distance, Donovan could tell they weren't from around this part of Ireland, maybe not from Ireland at all. The foreign looking ones were quieter than the gypsies, he noted. They didn't sing or dance, though they were drinking just as hard.

He hurried Gavin to finish the loading.

SARAH HAD HOPED there would be another market going on. She rode slowly down the main street, keeping her eye on the group of rowdies at the end of it by a large tent. All the storefronts were either boarded up or smashed. The few cars she'd seen two months back when she spoke with Julie were now vandalized beyond any kind of value. She resisted the temptation to pull her gun out and ride down the street demanding information.

If she didn't find somebody to talk to about where Julie lived, how was she going to find David? Had she truly waited all this time to finally come to Balinagh—putting her son at risk back at the rental cottage—all for nothing?

The frustration coursed through her until she wanted to scream. Her eyes flitted to both sides of the street for any possible indication that there was someone who could help her. She looked at the far end of the street where the gypsies were gathered and where she felt herself drawn to.

There were only five of them. They looked like thugs and so far, they hadn't seen her. Sarah decided to stay mounted in case she needed to make a run for it although the thought of galloping across miles of snowy pasture with fences and stonewalls hidden from view did not sound like a good plan.

She walked closer to them.

Seamus had been able to get the drop on three armed men, she thought, because they did not fear him. Like him, her greatest protection was their arrogance.

"BLIMEY, Da. Is she barking? What the hell is she doing?"

Donovan stopped stacking and stared with his mouth open at the sight of Sarah riding down the main street. "I have absolutely no idea," he said.

AT THE LAST MINUTE, Sarah slid off her horse and led him into a small alley off the street. She peered around the corner to see if the gypsies had seen her. They gave no indication of it. Taking in a long breath, she loosely tied Dan by his reins to a stunted tree in the alley and touched her gun in her shoulder harness.

I can do this, she thought.

She crept out of the alley and slid forward one careful yard at a time until she was a hundred feet away from them. One of the men shouted. The rest of them laughed. A skinny redheaded gypsy boy with badly crossed eyes took a step off the wooden walkway into the street. He was grinning broadly and looked very drunk. A glazed look came over his face. He dropped to his knees and vomited down the front of himself. The rest of the men roared with laughter.

Was she really looking at this rabble as a credible source of information? They were drunk. Anything they might say would probably be useless to her.

She watched one of the men stumble backwards on the wooden steps that led to what had been a restaurant a few months ago. He fell down to shrieks of laughter and rowdy insults from his friends.

Two of the men began shoving each other until one hauled off and slugged the other in the face. The rest of the group turned their attention to the grappling fighters, now on their hands and knees in the street. Sarah used the opportunity to back away a little bit since it was clear the gang was becoming more and more out of control. The nonfighting men alternately swore and cheered the fighters on. One of the fighters grabbed a piece of wood and began hammering away at his opponent which drove the gathered crowd wild with delight.

Sarah watched in horror as it became clear that the man intended to murder the other man, clearly inebriated, in the middle of the street. She watched the melee helplessly when, without warning, a pair of strong hands grabbed her from behind and jerked her sharply backwards.

The last thing she remembered seeing before a large dirty hand clapped over her face and eyes was the gypsy she had shot coming out of the restaurant.

He was wearing the University of Florida sweatshirt she had last seen on her husband.

19

S arah's hands would not stop shaking.

Even after Mike Donovan gave her a second mug of tea laced with whisky and checked the window for the third time to make sure the gypsies were still occupied, she could not make her hands stop trembling.

"I don't know what I was expecting," she said, cupping the hot mug in both hands. "Dear God, I really thought I was going to find David." She looked at Donovan and her eyes filled with tears. "Alive. It never...it never really occurred to me—" She shook her head.

"Drink your tea," Donovan said quietly. He looked at his son who stood in the corner of the abandoned store and was peering out the window onto the street.

Donovan had crept up quietly behind her when the fight broke out and hustled her into the building around the corner from where the gypsy men were gathered. Gavin had led her horse into the store too. In case the gypsies weren't quite as drunk as they looked, it wouldn't do to have it tied up outside where it might be seen. Donovan had just enough tea left in his thermos for a last cup. It was Gavin who had thought to find an unbroken mug from the store shelves.

Sarah looked at her horse that had just made a healthy deposit in one of the aisles of the small store.

What kind of nightmare am I living? she wondered.

"I'm sorry, missus," Donovan said. "We'll be able to leave as soon as it gets dark. They're pretty done for. I wouldn't expect any trouble from them soon."

"Except they're not all of 'em there," Gavin said from the window. "Or even the worst of 'em. You know that, Da."

"Shirrup, Gavin," Donovan said. He turned back to Sarah. "What is your interest in them?" he asked.

Sarah looked at him with eyes so full of pain and sadness it was all he could do not to look away.

"I thought they might have information about my husband. They had his horse. Plus, I...I wounded a gypsy that came to my place to steal my horses."

"Cor, Da! She's talking about Finn. She's the one shot him."

"Is that true?" Donovan asked her.

"I killed one of them," she said, staring directly into his eyes. "He tried to hurt my son."

Donovan nodded.

"Do you know them?" she asked.

"The man you wounded is the leader of this band of thugs," Donovan said. "His name is Finn. He's been a worthless piece of shite from the beginning. Lived with his extended family around these parts as gypsies do—under bridges, in caravans and tents. Was involved in petty theft stuff up to now and some senseless killing of dogs and cats.

"Been in prison for some years recently for robbing a grocer's with a weapon, I heard. But since the blackout, he's taken advantage of the situation. Come in to his own, ye might say. A natural leader is our Finn. And he's found a following of scum just like him."

"Three of his gang tried to kill Seamus McClenny yesterday," Sarah said. "They acted like they'd done it before. One of 'em said this guy Finn was looking for me. I guess to get revenge for shooting him."

"And for the other."

"The other?"

"I think the one you killed was Finn's brother, Ardan."

Sarah stood up and set her mug down. "I have to get back," she said.

Donovan held out a hand as if to restrain her. "Whoa, missus, that is not a good idea."

Sarah put her hands to her head as if she'd just experienced a terrible headache. "Stop...calling me 'missus.' My name is Sarah." She moved past him to where Dan was dozing.

"Look, Sarah, you can't leave." Donovan moved to put himself between her and the horse. "I don't have to tell you, I'm sure, how dangerous that lot is." He gestured in the direction of the window.

"They're a murderin' lot, so they are," Gavin added and received a glower from his father.

"I have to get home to my son," Sarah said. As she said the words, a terrible fear seized her and her sentence finished in a near shriek. "I have to get to my boy."

The thought came to her suddenly: *He's all I have left.*

"Sarah, please," Donovan said. "I'll be asking you to take a breath and think for a moment. Going out there now is *not* the most direct route to getting back to your lad."

"Not a-tall," Gavin said, shaking his head. "But it looks like they're packing up, Da. They're leaving the one poor bastard just lying in the road."

"Likely dead," Donovan said. He turned to Sarah. "Give them ten minutes to clear out and then you can be on your way. Gavin'll go with you."

"I will?" Gavin said happily. "Crackin'."

Sarah just wanted to be on her way home. She wanted it so bad it was all she could do not to mount Dan right there in the store.

"Fine," she said between gritted teeth.

Donovan moved over to the window to where Gavin stood.

"Take her home," he said to the boy, "and wait for me. Understand? Bunk down in the barn or wherever she's got an extra place but don't leave until I get there."

"When are you coming, then?"

Donovan looked back at Sarah who had Dan's reins in her hands now and was checking his girth.

"I'll get back home and see if a few of the lads will come with me. But don't look for us until tomorrow."

"You really think Finn'll come to her place, Da?"

"I'm surprised he hasn't done it before now. Let's just pray we still have time before he gets there." He turned away from Gavin to address Sarah. "Can ye tell me how Seamus escaped the three thugs to tell the story?"

Sarah led Dan to the door and jerked back a curtain to get a better view of the street.

"He shot them," she said, dropping the curtain.

"He...shot them? All?"

Sarah pulled out her Glock and checked to see that it was chambered and ready.

"Yes. All," she said.

"And this was two days ago?"

Sarah looked into the distance and her gaze seemed to glaze over.

"No," she said, her voice barely above a whisper. "Yesterday."

Donovan had a bad feeling about the timing of all this. He turned back to his son.

"Go on, get going," he said. "I'll be there before nightfall."

. . .

THE RIDE from Balinagh normally took two hours with a combination of walking and trotting. As soon as Sarah was remounted, she put Dan into a canter that spilled into a gallop before they were half mile outside the village. She could hear Gavin's pleas for her to wait but she couldn't.

She just couldn't.

As she rode, she scanned the hills for any sign of life that might signal an ambush, mostly she was so panicked about getting back to the cottage to see for herself that John was safe that she couldn't really think about anything else.

In fact, her focused, maniacal determination worked to block out the other thing.

David.

Sarah closed her legs around Dan and urged him faster. The horse felt like a powder keg of energy and force beneath her. His gallop carried them towards home with very little prompting from her—as if he'd been waiting for her all along to let him go all out.

As she thundered down the wet road that led from Balinagh to their cottage, Sarah never thought for a moment that the horse might slip, or that she might lose her balance. It was simply not conceivable that he would do anything but fly over the potholes and swivel around the sharp turns in the road, just not believable that she might do anything but ride him as fast and sure as if she'd been born to do it.

And if, as she would later wonder, everything in her life before this moment was somehow just preparing her to meet this spasm of incredible need, she would've considered it a life well lived.

The feel of the rhythmic, thundering hooves as she galloped and the cold wind stinging her face mixed with her conviction that she would...she must...find John safe. The ride would end with her arms around her child, holding him snugly to her heart.

Time enough later—much, much later—to talk to him about

his Dad. For now, she had to get back to him. The intensity of the craving to see him again was as vital and elementary as the need to take her next breath.

She was only a mile from home when she slowed Dan to a walk—just to catch her breath, and to give him a moment to gather himself for the mad gallop down the main drive of the cottage. It wouldn't do to kill the poor horse and have to run the rest of the way on foot.

She didn't expect to be able to see any sign of the cottage from this distance. In the two other times she'd walked or ridden back from the village and strained for that first, welcoming sign— usually a thin needle of smoke to indicate a fire in the hearth— she'd never caught a sign of the cottage for at least another half mile or more.

Which is why, when she saw the long funnel of black smoke jutting up into the sky above where she knew the cottage should be she sat up suddenly straight in the saddle, stopping her horse dead in the road.

The cottage was burning.

20

Sarah dug her heels hard into Dan's side and the horse bolted from a walk into a gallop. She never saw the ground rushing by beneath her in a blur of green and brown or the two small stonewalls that she and the horse vaulted over as easily as if they'd been puddles on a street. Her eyes strained to see the cottage appear on the horizon over the next hill. She willed the house to materialize intact and the smoke, which grew blacker the closer she came, to dissipate to reveal that the cottage still stood.

When she crested the final hill on the homeward drive to the cottage, she sucked in a hard breath. The sound more than anything startled her horse, who shied violently, nearly unseating her. And she never took her eyes off the sight at the end of the hill: the little cottage, fully engulfed in flames, and the forecourt pocked with lifeless bodies scattered like sacks of grain carelessly dropped from a wagon.

Her energy seeped from her. Her nearly maniacal urgency to be at the cottage gave way to an involuntary hesitancy to confirm her worst suspicions. Was it hope or certainty that she would find him safe that had fueled her on the crazy gut-wrenching ride from Balinagh? Her weight rested solidly in the saddle as she surveyed the terrible scene below. And Dan came to a halt.

She tried to control her breathing as she watched the forecourt with the motionless bodies and the raging fire. A part of her almost believed she could feel the heat. She stared, stunned and paralyzed. A sound came from just over her left shoulder but she didn't turn.

Gavin was laboring up the hill with his horse and wagon.

"Cor, Missus," he said, gasping for breath as if he'd run alongside the horses himself. "You nearly gave me a heart attack."

His words shook her out of the moment and she gathered her reins in her hands and pushed Dan down the hill with her legs. Once she was moving, she allowed herself to think the impossible: *maybe he was still alive.* The thought galvanized her into a full gallop down the hill toward the cottage, the appalled shouts of Gavin ringing in her ears behind her.

She dismounted before Dan even downshifted out of the canter. The closer she got to the cottage, she could see that many of the lifeless forms were animals—mostly their sheep. From the looks of it, all of them.

Sarah stepped over several carcasses, each one mottled bright red against the dirty white of their wool, and went to the dead man lying face down in the center of the courtyard. Her gun in her hand, she made a quick scan of the forecourt before touching him. She knelt and turned him over.

It was Seamus, his blue eyes open and unseeing, his throat cut in a bloodless white arc. Tears welled up in her eyes. She got a flashback of Seamus walking with John across the forecourt to the barn, his gait stooped and halting, his large hand resting lightly on her boy's shoulder. She closed his eyes and saw her hand was shaking.

Sarah felt the heat from the inferno at her back as she jumped up to run to the stable. She jerked open the door but the barn was empty except for the bodies of the two little goats that had helped sustain them for the weeks and months since they had arrived.

The sight of the little dead goats, for some reason, triggered a feeling of blinding rage in Sarah. She left the barn and ran to the paddock. It was empty except for more dead sheep.

"John!" she screamed, her eyes raking the entrance to the pasture and the little back courtyard outside the kitchen door. "John Matthew!"

Gavin brought the wagon into the forecourt but his horses panicked at the proximity of the fire and he fought to keep them calm. He leapt out, grabbed their bridles and led them to the far side of the barn, all the while looking over his shoulder at the carnage and the dead body in the middle of the courtyard.

Sarah approached the cottage. One of John's dogs lay dead in her path.

Quickly, Gavin unhooked the horses from the wagon, pushed them into the barn—not bothering to find a stall—and shut the door. He ran to Sarah who was kneeling by the little dog and looking at the burning cottage, her face a mask of unreadable agony.

"Missus," he said, breathlessly, "they'll have taken the lad."

She didn't take her eyes off the burning cottage.

"*This* is what they do," she said tonelessly.

"No, they won't have burned him in there," Gavin said. He touched her arm gingerly. "You weren't here when they came, so they'll have taken him with them."

A look of hope flashed across her face and she turned to him.

He nodded. "I'm sure of it." He looked at the burning house as a large piece of timber came crashing down in front of them, making them both take a step back. "He's not in there."

Sarah looked back at the cottage and then at the dead puppy on the ground. She shook her head.

"There's also a woman," she said. "Dierdre."

"Mrs. McClenny?" Gavin looked back at Seamus lying on the

ground. "Aye, well." He shook his head and looked at the cottage. "That's not good."

THERE WAS nothing they could do for the cottage but let it burn. They had nothing with which to put out the flames and it was too dangerous to attempt to retrieve any belongings from inside. Gavin went back to the horses, Dan included, and untacked and fed them. He put each of them in stalls, dragged the dead goats and the sheep to a small trench behind the barn, and began digging a larger trench for Seamus.

Sarah sat in the unharnessed wagon as if in a trance and watched the cottage burn. What sun there had ever been that day had long disappeared behind a cloud, not to return. She held the gun in her hands, tracing the lines, the numbers, the indentations on it like one would a treasured talisman. Her eyes never left the cottage.

She watched the outline of the porch crumble and she remembered sitting out on those steps just three months ago with David. She remembered watching the stars from those steps, and the feel of his warm lips on hers. Her eyes travelled to the chimney that jutted from the middle of the little cottage and she remembered the nights spent sitting around its hearth, the three of them laughing, playing cards, telling stories.

The frame around the smaller living room window in front gave way and broke into pieces on the ground. She expected to see angry tongues of flame emerge but instead, a plume of grey smoke belched out into the early evening air. As she watched, she realized she was praying. Praying for guidance, for relief from pain, for hope that her boy was alive.

She heard Gavin speaking from around the side of the barn but she couldn't understand his words. He must have been speaking to her, she didn't know. She had been staring at the house for a good ten minutes before she realized it had started to rain. She'd lived in Ireland so long she hardly noticed the sudden downpours any more. She watched as the flames slowly died and the air turned to a thick, stagnant layer of black fog.

She leaned over the side of the wagon and threw up into the bushes.

In all her nightmares of worry back home in the States about what could happen to her child, she had never come close to imagining the terror and agony of what she had experienced in the last hour. And while she lived with hope that, as Gavin suggested, John was *not* in the burning house, the knowledge that that meant he was with the murderous gypsies was nearly as unendurable.

She held the gun to her chest like it had the power to change things. She finished her prayers with the plea to God Almighty that He keep John safe, and that He help him say and do the right things while the gypsies had him to keep him alive, and that He help Sarah navigate the rest of this unfathomable nightmare.

Gavin spoke to her again, this time louder and closer. He was saying something about the rain and how, Saints be praised, it had come at a divine moment. Sarah couldn't take her eyes off the cottage. They were coming to a moment, she knew, when the rain would put out the fire completely and allow them to enter the cottage. And then they would know for sure.

...And then they would know.

"Missus?"

Sarah dragged her eyes from the smoldering building to look at Gavin. He looked tired and filthy. His face was black from the soot of the fire and sweat and rain and created rivulets down both his cheeks. It made him look like he'd been crying.

"I've built a wee fire," he said, indicating with a jerk of his head the backcourt on the side of the barn. "The root cellar's not been touched by the fire so I'll check to see if there's anything we can use to eat. Is that all right?"

Sarah shifted in her position in the wagon to look back at the house.

John was hungry all the time, too, she thought.

"Fine," she said dully.

"Me Da will be here soon. Maybe in an hour or so."

Sarah didn't respond so Gavin turned to find the root cellar.

She bowed her head and finished her prayers. It was all she could do.

When she heard the shout, she stood up so fast that the gun dropped to the floorboard of the wagon. Instead of snatching it up, she left it there and jumped to the ground, facing the direction of Gavin's shout.

Something inside her just knew.

He came running from around the corner of the barn. In the fading light of the day, she saw him run toward her, his arms pumping at his side, his head up, his eyes locked onto hers.

"Mom!"

And that was when she started to weep. When he launched himself into her open arms, she crushed him so tightly to her that he squeaked and still she cried. She kissed his tousled brown hair, his filthy, tear-streaked cheeks, his sweet little-boy mouth that was talking and exclaiming all at once.

Thank you, God. Dear Lord in Heaven, thank you, thank you.

THEY FOUND Dierdre in the house.

John told them that Seamus had made him run and hide in the root cellar when they heard the gypsies come. He had one of the puppies with him but couldn't find the other. Seamus told him he'd come for him when it was all clear.

"But he never came, Mom."

Seamus's plan was for Dierdre to hold them off with the guns from inside the house. Then Seamus was to provide a distraction outside, facing down the gypsies, so that John could slip out the back.

"You're a brave lad, young John," Donovan said, nodding at John. "You're da would be proud."

John nodded solemnly, but Sarah could tell Mike's words were a balm to him. Donovan had come not forty minutes after John was found. He'd brought with him ten other people, five of them able-bodied men and the rest women and children.

Donovan had wasted no time in clearing away the dead animal carcasses and bringing some order to the devastation. His men found what remained of poor Dierdre. They buried both her and Seamus that very night. Afterward, it was too late to do anything but build a campfire and create a bit of shelter against the night. His people pitched their tents in the paddock and set up their bedrolls in the barn. The women, silent as phantoms, prepared steaming pots of small-animal stew that simmered on black rocks in the campfires.

Sarah could not take her eyes off John. She watched him hungrily as he walked the camp, staying mostly with Donovan and Gavin. Her preference would have been to keep him wrapped in her arms. Her terror was too newly lived to be discounted by the fact of his existence. She now knew the sharp agony of the terrible loss of him and it was even worse than she'd ever imagined. Her joy to have him delivered back to her was tempered by the knowledge of how vulnerable they all were.

David.

She closed her eyes in exhaustion and held her hands to her face. She jerked her head up to see where John might be and discovered that Donovan had quietly sat down next to her.

"Whoa, didn't mean to startle you," he said. He was holding out a metal cup to her.

"You didn't," Sarah said. "I just..." She shook her head and nodded toward where John and Gavin squatted near the fire. "I'm just never going to feel safe again."

She drank from the cup without thinking. It was some kind of homemade alcohol and burned all the way down her throat. The pain felt good and almost instantly she felt some of the edge of the day creep away.

"Nor none of us, that's the truth," Donovan said with a heavy sigh. "I am so sorry we didn't get here in time."

Sarah turned to look at him.

"What a nice man you are," she said.

That made him smile and he took a pull from a flask he'd been holding in his hand.

"You brought all these people here to help us." She took another sip and let the alcohol do its work. She closed her eyes, willing the drink to calm her and not open up the floodgates of emotion as was all too likely.

"Well, to be honest, we're family, you see," he said. "All of us related in some way."

One of the women approached. She wore baggy jeans and a tired smile. Her hair was gathered back in a single braid down her back. She handed Sarah a bowl of stew and a dented spoon.

"You'll be hungry," she said.

Sarah glimpsed over the woman's shoulder at John who was eating and laughing with Gavin. She shook her head in wonder and accepted the bowl.

"Thank you," she said. "Thank you for everything."

"Sure, it's nothing," the woman said. "I'm Fiona, Mike's big sister." The woman knelt down across from Sarah. "We've heard a good bit about you from Siobhan and the others. It's a pleasure to finally meet you."

"I guess we're famous," Sarah said. She spooned into the stew. "Those crazy Americans—coming to the remotest point on the globe so they can give up electronics and live the simple life."

Fiona frowned. "Sure, I'm not positive we are the remotest point on the globe," she said wryly.

"Sorry," Sarah said. "I didn't mean it like that."

"Fi's just giving you a hard time," Donovan said, frowning at his sister.

Fiona ignored him. "Has Mike told you the news yet?"

Sarah snapped her head to look at Donovan. "What news?"

"Can you not let the woman have two mouthfuls before agitating her?" Donovan said to his sister.

"There's news?" Sarah repeated.

Donovan sighed. "Now's as good a time to give it, I guess." He jerked his head at Fiona. "Gather the others. I don't want to say this twice."

Fiona picked up Sarah's bowl from the ground where she'd laid it, winked at Sarah and left.

"Is it good news?"

"Were you expecting good news?" he said.

"I...I guess...I'm always hopeful..." Sarah was at a loss for words.

"That maybe help was coming?" Donovan asked. "That any day now the Irish government would roll up with an aid truck busting full of food and jam, or that they'd get busy replacing the power lines?"

"Well, yes, actually."

Donovan shook his head.

"Look, before the others get here I need to know what you want to do about the problems you've had here." He glanced in the direction of the burnt house, now just a black shadow towering eerily in the background.

"What I intend to do?" she repeated.

"I mean, I assume you will be coming with us? There's no real need to stay now, is there? Your animals are gone, your house is gone."

The unspoken phrase echoed in Sarah's head: *Your husband is gone.*

"You should come with us," he said. "We're building a community. We'll watch each other's backs and plant food and rebuild our little patch of the country. It will be safer for you with us. There's a place for you and your lad if you want to come."

"I can't leave," Sarah said.

"For the love of God, why not?" Donovan sputtered in frustration. "You have nothing left here. Will you be living out of the *barn*? Why would you stay?"

"Because," Sarah said, her voice as steely and flat as the heart that beat in her breast, "the bastards will be back." She looked at Donovan. "And this time I'll be ready for them."

Now it was Donovan's turn to stare.

"You *want* them to come?" he said, his face twisted in confusion.

"I don't understand you," Sarah said, standing up and brushing the dirt from her jeans. "They've destroyed my home, threatened my child, possibly murdered my husband and definitely murdered my friends and I'm supposed to *walk away*? I don't know how you do things in Ireland, but we are not finished here. Not by a long shot."

After a pause, Donovan broke into a wild laugh that had the approaching group of men and women walk even faster toward them.

"You're crazy," he said. "And you have fulfilled every myth I ever had about how Americans think. It really isn't just the movies, is it? This is how you Yanks really are."

He turned to the crowd who gathered around him.

"Alright, listen up. I've got news and it's not pretty."

Sarah looked at the group of men and women standing in the forecourt of her holiday cottage. They were ragged and thin and not terribly clean but their eyes were bright and intent.

They're survivors, she thought. *Good people to have with you in a fight.*

One of the women held a baby in her arms and Sarah was amazed to realize that the baby must have been born after the incident. *Without electricity or doctors or formula or baby monitors.* She smiled at the young mother.

John wriggled out of the crowd and came to stand next to her and slip his hand into hers. For him to do it in front of everyone, she realized, meant he must be feeling insecure about what Donovan was about to reveal. She squeezed his hand and brought her full attention back to Mike.

"We now know what happened," Donovan said. "And knowing it helps us. It helps to know how long we'll likely need to live like this."

There were several gasps from the group. Mike held up his hands for quiet.

"Like I said, it's not good news, but knowledge is power and we'll do well to remember that." He took a deep breath, glanced at Sarah, and began.

"David Cahill's boy, Craig, made it to Limerick and back and he's brought us news, so he has, about what happened. Now, Craig's not here to tell you himself because he sustained some injuries on the road and he...well, he's passed as a result. So we'll be thankful to young Craig and the good Lord above for letting him get back home before He claimed him."

The group murmured and Sarah felt her anxiety ratchet up as she waited.

"Basically, what happened was this," Donovan said. "There was a nuclear bomb dropped by some unidentified terrorist group over London four months back. I don't know all the gigawatts and gaggo-rays of what happened or why they didn't just drop the bomb right *on* London and be done with it but it seems exploding it up in the air was even worse. And since we've all been affected by it, that would seem to be right." Donovan took a deep breath as if he were still processing the information for himself.

"The nuclear explosion basically took out everything in the UK that was electronic. And since all our cars, our phones, our computers, and our power grid use electronics to run, the bastards basically bombed us back to the Stone Age and that's the simple truth of it."

One of the men stepped forward.

"Is it true the cities are radioactive like they said at first?"

Donovan shook his head. "A rumor. Not at-tall."

We could have left, Sarah thought. *It would've been safe to leave after all.*

"When are they going to fix it, then?"

"Well, Craig said the Brits have their hands full with their own country and then they'll think about helping us."

"Typical."

"Plus," and here he turned to look at Sarah, "A nonnuclear missile destroyed a good part of Boston. That'll be what most of us saw on the TV last September. Where did you say your folks lived, Sarah?"

John spoke up, his voice shaking. "Florida."

Donovan nodded. "If what Craig said is correct, the American south is fine."

"Thank God," Sarah whispered, tears welling in her eyes. "Washington?" she asked.

"It appears it was targeted but the bomb went off course and detonated over the Atlantic."

"Incompetent idiots," someone shouted.

Donovan addressed the man who spoke. "Maybe. But from where I'm standing, competent enough."

"How long to rebuild?" someone asked.

"They're working on that now," Mike replied.

"Our country will help you," John said.

Donovan turned to him and the effort it took to smile seemed to weigh him down.

"Your country is helping its friend England first," he said.

He listened to the general agreement from the crowd before speaking again.

"The point of how this new information affects all of us here is this..." He paused for a moment to make sure he had their attention. "Now we know for sure *there is no one coming*. We are on our own and likely to be for years to come."

21

"Dad was right."

John was trying to make his dog, Patrick, remain in the *stay* position. He would walk away from the dog but when he turned around, he was always right behind him. Sarah sat watching him, a cup of steaming black tea in her hands. She had just been thinking about possibly preparing John for bad news about his father and wondering how much she should say.

"What do you mean?"

"About what happened. He said it was mostly likely an EMP."

"You're right," Sarah said. "He did say that."

John pointed a finger at the dog. "I said, *stay*, Patrick! I read about electromagnetic pulses in my *Science News*," he said. "It, basically, like, shoots out a wave of gamma radiation in all directions—kinda like the electrical storms we get in Jacksonville during the summer? Only it wipes out everything electrical."

John released the puppy from the command and sat down next to Sarah in the dirt. "Dad called it."

The dog collapsed into John's lap, nipping and licking at the boy's sleeve.

"Why didn't you say something last night at the campfire?"

"Seriously? Mom." Her son looked at her as if she were being deliberately dense. "Adults don't like smart-alecky kids makin' 'em feel stupid."

John used his finger to dig gunk out of his dog's eyes before wiping it on his pant leg.

"People like Mr. Donovan don't care *why* something happened, only *that* it happened. Me, I like to know *why*. Dad does, too." He shrugged.

Sarah smiled at him. "How old are you again?"

John looked up from his dog. "Mom, now that everybody's here, we're gonna go look for Dad, right?"

Sarah looked at him. "I'm just not sure where to start," she said. "No one has even heard of this Julie person..."

"You're giving up?" John stopped brushing his dog.

"No, of course not, John. We'll continue to look for him but..."

How to say this? How to say "prepare yourself for the worse?" Was there any point in even saying that until the worst was actually confirmed?

"But what?"

"No buts. Sorry, sweetie." She reached over and drew him to her.

It was true what they said about the resiliency of children, Sarah thought. Like a lot of parents, she had worried about so many unimportant things in the past. When she thought of her concerns—*concerns that actually kept her up at night!*—about whether she should allow him to play football or if they should tell him his hamster died, she wanted to laugh outloud.

Her concerns now centered on his very survival. And as for staying awake at night with her worries, she was too exhausted at the end of the long days. One thing she had learned: the coming day would take care of the coming day. If nothing else, that was a lesson that was ground into her head, her heart, her very bones.

She watched as John jumped up and tossed a stick to the dog.

She knew how much it hurt him to lose the other dog, and how worried he was about his Dad. As Sarah watched him, she found herself marveling at how quickly he'd let go of the old ways and his old life. For him, that was then. This is now. And it was that simple.

She suddenly realized how, in just a few short months, her son had morphed from a pampered child dependent on his electronics for amusement to a self-reliant boy comfortably adapting to a new world order that involved physical labor as well as cunning to survive.

"We'll never stop trying," she said.

"Until we find him," he said, turning in her arms until they both faced the blacked hulk of their former cottage.

"That's right," she said, her voice catching with emotion. "Until we find him."

So badly did she want to believe it, her heart literally ached in her chest.

Dear God, had she really lost David forever? How was that possible? They had only gone on vacation.

LATER THAT AFTERNOON, Sarah sat in one of the wagons parked on the perimeter of the camp and wiped down the Glock with a rag. She didn't really know what she was doing but it made her feel like she was preparing in some way for the fight ahead. Fiona approached with two cups of tea.

"May I join you?"

"Of course, please do."

Sarah moved over to give her room.

"I just wanted to say, I'm sorry for all your troubles," Fiona said, settling in on the wooden seat next to Sarah. "Mike told me you plan on staying here so you can fight the gypsies when they come back."

"Sound a little nuts when you put it like that."

"He says you're hoping we'll stay and help you fight them."

"I can't do it alone. I mean, it would be good for all of us, Fiona. You can't start a new community looking over your shoulder." She pointed to the blackened hulk of the cottage. "They'll just come do this to you eventually."

"Possibly. But not straightaway."

Sarah shrugged. "You're here now. Why not end it now?"

"And then, afterward, you intend to come with us?"

"I...where is it you're going? Mike wasn't too specific."

"We are creating a community, possibly somewhere close to the sea since most of the men are fishermen."

"Why not stay where you were?"

"We're from all over. Most of us didn't own the land we lived on. And now the crisis has rewritten the rules of land ownership."

"I wouldn't be too sure of that," Sarah said. "I mean, you don't expect the laws to return? Trust me, the McKinneys will collect on the insurance on this place before the year is out."

"I hope you're right, but I doubt it."

"So you're betting that this chaos is permanent?"

Fiona looked down at her hands and took her time answering. "We feel it's better to accept the worst," she said, "than to live our lives on hold, constantly waiting for something to happen that maybe never will."

Sarah wondered, *Was she referring to David?*

"So if you were to come with us," Fiona continued, "and I hope you do, we'll find a place where we can all live."

"And watch each other's backs."

"Well, that, sure, but also to enjoy each other too."

Sarah had already seen and admired how the group seemed to take pleasures from the simplest things. With Mike at the helm, it would definitely be a well-organized and judiciously run community.

"We'll come, of course," Sarah said. "And with thanks. I'm grateful to have found family."

"I'm glad," Fiona said. "I was hoping you would."

"Now that we're sisters, can I ask you a question?"

Fiona grinned. "Shoot," she said.

"What happened to Gavin's mother?"

"That would be Mike's Ellen," Fiona said. "She died when the boy was five."

"How?"

"A riding accident. She was brilliant, so she was. Nobody better with horses around these parts and that's saying something."

"She fell?"

Fiona nodded. "In a competition. The horse shied at something. She came off but got right back on and finished the course. Went to bed that night. Never woke up. Mike loved her something fierce. Probably still does. But there you are."

Sarah watched Mike as he directed the men to tighten a canvas drape over one of the campfire cook stoves.

"Yeah," she said, watching him work. "There we are."

THE LITTLE GROUP kept well away from the burnt house, not least because wisps of ash and soot sprang up at every breeze from the blackened grave and clung to any nearby face or bit of clothing. A large cook fire had been constructed in the middle of the forecourt with bedding in the barn and a half circle of small tents in the adjacent paddock. While there were ten people in all, Sarah counted only five men. Estimates of the gypsies numbers ranged wildly between fifty to more than a hundred.

As Fiona and the other women worked to cook a meal over the open fire, Sarah slipped into the barn. The gypsies had killed most of the livestock except for the two ponies, Star and Ned, who had been in the pasture.

Sarah went to Dan's stall and he walked over to greet her. She patted him on the neck. Just seeing his big brown eyes, filled her with a kind of comfort.

"Hey, boy, you doing okay?"

He nickered in response and she held his face in her hands and looked into his eyes. His lashes were long and he regarded her sleepily. She touched the velvety softness of his nose as he blew warm breath into her hands.

"You came through for me yesterday, big guy," she said quietly. "You got me here when I needed you to, as sure footed and fast as Secretariat himself." She patted his neck. "I don't know why I think so but somehow I don't think I could do any of this without you."

"Ahhh, don't be giving me a reason to kill the poor beast."

The unexpected voice made both Sarah and Dan jump, even though Donovan showed himself before he finished speaking.

"You scared the life out of me," Sarah said, turning to him with a grin. "What are you doing in here?"

Donovan shrugged. "Probably same as you. Having a moment to meself before all hell breaks loose."

Sarah turned back to her horse.

"I talked to Fi this morning," she said. "She told me a little bit more about the community y'all are starting. You know, Mike, I hate the thought of putting your family in danger. I wish I could make you understand why I feel like I need to."

"It's easy enough to understand," Mike said, leaning on the half door of the stall. "They killed Dierdre and Seamus. You want revenge."

"That's not it," Sarah said, her finger tightening around Dan's mane. "I'm afraid for my life. For my son's life." She turned and looked at him. "I can't live with the threat of them surprising us. I can't live like that."

"If you live with us," Donovan said, "in a community, you won't need to. You'll be protected. That's what communities do."

"And I would like that," she said, looking into his eyes. "I absolutely want that. But it doesn't take away the threat. Look," she said, joining him where he stood in the aisle of the barn, "If you had wolves attacking your sheep, would you remove the threat or just put the sheep in a bigger flock?"

"That's asinine," he said, his eyes locking onto hers.

"It's the same thing."

"It's not at-tall the same thing."

"Tell me how it isn't! You say 'don't upset the wolves, and they'll leave you alone.' I say, 'kill the wolves and hang their molding, stinking carcasses on pikes by the front gate as a warning to other wolves.'"

Donovan looked at her and then burst out laughing.

"Remind me," he said, wiping his eyes, "is it an American Soccer Mom you are or a Chicago hit man? I keep getting them confused and obviously you do, too."

Sarah laughed. "In America, we're all a little bit of both."

"And sure it's *not* the same thing," he said. And then, without warning, he leaned over and kissed her on the mouth.

Sarah, surprised, allowed the kiss for longer than she would've if he'd in any way telegraphed his intention. She finally pulled away and put her fingers to her lips.

"Mike, no," she said. "I can't."

Donovan took a step back.

"I am so sorry, Sarah," he said. "I swear I didn't know I was going to do that until I was doing it. Believe me..."

"I do, I do. It's okay, it's just..."

"No need to explain. Jaysus! And you still wondering if your husband is alive or dead. I don't know what came over me."

"Mike, it's okay. Really." Sarah touched him on his sleeve. "Let's forget it, okay? If the world was different, maybe if circumstances and they were different..."

"Now, now, none of that." Donovan waved away her words. "Best idea yet is to just forget it, if you can do that."

"I can."

"Cheers. Now, if you've checked on your gallant steed, we'll be seeing what delights Fiona has cooked up for our pleasure this evening." He held out his arm to usher her from the barn into the dying light of the early evening.

MACK FINN SAT, smoking a cigarette, in an old wooden rocking chair on the front porch. It was a good chair with a comfortable pad. Finn had spent nearly the full day in it, rocking, sipping tea and smoking. From the porch he had a good view of the whole camp and the long drive that led to the croft.

He watched as ten or so of his men transferred boxes from the two shabby horse-drawn wagons that stood in the middle of the old lady's vegetable garden next to the barn. Every once in awhile, one of the horses would dip its head to nibble at something on the ground.

They had found the farm abandoned a few days earlier. Maybe because they hadn't killed its inhabitants, Finn had decided to move in rather than put it to the torch. He decided it suited him, being a landowner. It occurred to him that he would be the first of his family not to live in a tent or a caravan. He wondered for a minute if he really cared about such things. He was now the oldest living person in his family, a family that went back hundreds of generations.

He recognized that he missed the girl Jules.

Everything had gone arseways so fast, he wasn't sure exactly *what* had happened. When the old woman was killed, Jules had gone mental. It was all he could do to protect himself from her. That was a shocker. Up to then, she'd been so sweet and gentle like. He hadn't meant to hurt her. But the stupid whore attacked him! It was her own fault. He was only defending himself.

"Oy, Mack!"

Finn didn't move his head but his eyes flickered to the young man who came to the porch.

"Brendan wants to know should we raid the kitchen or eat what we got in town. People are getting hungry." The gobshite looked nervous to Finn.

"What people?" Finn said. "You?"

The boy didn't speak.

"Where's the Yank?" Finn asked, leaning forward in his chair to see if he could spot him from the porch. "Is he talking?"

The boy nodded.

"Aye. He said he came here on holiday to fish. He said he came alone, like."

Finn stood up, flicked his cigarette butt into the bushes and abruptly walked off the porch. The farm was noisy with the antics of his men, some of them drunk, some fighting. He walked into the barn where two men were stacking boxes against a wall. They turned when he came in.

"Where's Brendan?" he asked.

A swarthy man in his forties jerked his head to indicate the other side of the long barn.

Finn strode down the barn, glancing with satisfaction at the half-full stalls. The family had taken their horses but had left behind full bales of stacked hay. The need to take care of possessions was a new feeling for Finn. He was used to just taking what he needed. He wasn't sure he liked the feeling of ownership. It made him feel anxious.

At the end of the barn, he exited the south entrance. There sat two men by a small stone-ringed campfire, the Yank and Brendan.

Brendan stood up at Finn's approach. "Hey, Guv," Brendan said easily. "Checking out your plantation?"

Finn ignored him. Brendan was a big man with the easy confidence that comes of towering over most people in daily interactions. It annoyed Finn that he never acted worried about him. The way Finn saw things, Brendan should be plenty worried about him.

The American looked up and, amazingly, smiled.

What the shite did he have to smile about? Finn wondered.

"Comfortable, I see?" he said to the Yank.

"I'm good," the Yank replied, pulling his worn blanket around him tighter as if to belie his words. It had been a cold afternoon and the evening promised to be even colder.

"So, just in Ireland on holiday, are ye?" Finn squatted next to the man and fished out a cigarette. Finn saw out of the corner of his eye that the American glanced at Brendan.

Finn thought to himself, *Oh, so it's like that, is it? Friends, are we?*

"Yes, I heard about the great fishing in this part of the country..."

"Oh, aye, we got great fishing here. Really great. So, how is it you ended up lashed to a bed by that harpy back yonder?"

"I was just helping her out," the man said. He looked bad but he'd rallied in the week since Mack's men had found him tied to a boat anchor in the back room of that hag's cottage. They'd nearly killed him, too, until all the noise from Julie, who was in complete hysterics over the murder of her mother—an unexpected bollocks—had brought Finn's attention to what they were about to do.

The Yank was his winning ticket to getting *her*. He hated to think how close he'd come to losing him because of those stupid gobshites.

"So you got enough to eat?" Finn stood up and stared down at the man. In many ways, the Yank didn't look any different from his men. He had a scruffy beard, filthy, ripped clothes and a look that vacillated between desperation and vacancy. But there was something else about him. Something settled and self-assured. The kind of something that came from money and having it all done for you your whole life.

The kind of something that Finn absolutely *hated*.

DAVID WATCHED the scruffy little gypsy walk away. He watched Finn rub his shoulder like it still hurt him. Likely, it still did. When he spoke, David could see the malignancy in his eyes, like a feral animal that wanted to rip and hurt just for the sake of it.

There's something really wrong with that guy, David found himself thinking.

The other gypsy, Brendan, eased back down onto the ground next to David and gave the little campfire a poke with a long stick.

"He's not buying yer shite, Yank," he said matter of factly.

David brought his hand to his face to massage his forehead tiredly.

"He knows she's yer wife, mate," Brendan insisted. "Why d'ya think yer still alive?"

"I don't know, man," David said. "I just know I am."

While Brendan assembled a mealy sandwich to share with him, David couldn't help but watch him in wonder.

He didn't think Brendan was the one who'd murdered Betta, but his hands were likely not clean. He'd been kind to David for reasons that David couldn't yet fathom. He couldn't help but feel grateful to the man but he also knew he needed to fight the feeling.

Brendan was operating with his own agenda and David's life or wellbeing played no role in it. He needed to regain his strength and try to use the big gypsy to his own ends—which meant separating his gratitude from his actions. The only thing that mattered now that he was still alive, was that he reunite with Sarah and John.

Brendan handed David the sandwich and David smiled at him in a perfect mime of typical American eager politeness.

"Thanks, man," he said. "I really appreciate everything you've done for me."

"No worries, Yank," Brendan said, smiling back at him.

THAT NIGHT at the evening meal, the group at Sarah's burned cottage sat around the open fire. Fiona seemed to be generally accepted as the one in charge of all things domestic—meals, the children, and the other women. Sarah could see that most of the women, with the exception of the young teenaged niece of Mike and Fiona who was also the unwed mother, were the wives of Donovan's men. So far, the extent of their contact with Sarah was to smile shyly at her.

Mike sat next to her on a log rolled up to the fire. He held two plates of stewed lamb and soda bread and offered her one.

"At least it's not squirrel again," he said, his eyes watching the perimeter of the small camp as he spoke.

Sarah took the plate and tore off a piece of the still-warm bread.

"Fiona's a miracle maker to be able to create these meals out of virtually nothing," she said with amazement.

"Fiona's a good girl," Mike said absently. "Your boy doing okay?"

Sarah appreciated his question but knew there was more to it.

"I guess I've been acting pretty clingy with him lately," she admitted.

"No, no," he said, looking at her. "Not at-tall. No more than any sane mother would who had just experienced thirty minutes of believing her bairn to be murdered. Not at-tall."

Sarah looked away to hide the emotion stinging her eyes.

Would she ever get over those thirty minutes? Could any mother?

"But we'll be needing to talk about your problem with the gypsies now."

Sarah put her plate down and decided to choose her words carefully. "It is my belief, Mike," she said, "that it is not just *my* problem. I mean, unless you think you can live with them somehow."

"I'm not thinking that."

"But you do think that by defying them or calling attention to yourselves you'll make it worse?"

"Aye. Something like that."

Sarah heard first and then saw John across the campfire laughing at something Gavin said. She watched the older boy scoop her son up and the two playfully wrestle in the dirt before Fiona shooed them away from the fire.

"*Ejeet* boy will never grow up," Mike muttered, watching them too.

"I guess that's what this new world is all about," Sarah said. "Growing up fast. I've seen it in John and hated to see it at the same time I was glad for it."

Mike looked back at her and smiled.

"You're like no Irish woman I ever knew," he said.

"How so?" Sarah picked her plate back up. "Don't tell me about being strong or resilient or crap like that, because I warn you. I've seen Fiona in action so I wouldn't buy it."

"No, it's not that. Ireland is full of strong women. With the drunken bums many Irish men are, they've had to be. It's not that. Being tough is one thing, but doing it with your...your..."

"Swagger?" Sarah laughed. "Trust me, all American women have a little bit of John Wayne in them. It's part of our culture."

"Aye, must be."

Sarah watched the other men sitting around the campfire. There were those two, not counting Gavin. Two more were patrolling the perimeter of the camp and would, in shifts, all night long.

"All right then," Mike said, collecting her empty plate. "I have a bit of news for you that probably won't change your mind about waiting for the gypsies to come kill us all but I need to tell you."

"News? Where did you get more news?"

Instantly, Sarah tried to locate John with her eyes. She needed to see him before the landscape changed yet again.

"Same place I got the first bit, Aidan Kinney. He's one of 'em's that's on watch tonight. He'd neglected to tell me a bit of information he picked up in town. Didn't think it was important until he got to talking with his wife last night about you."

"About me?"

"Well, really, just about you being American and all."

"He heard something about David."

Sarah felt a huge chasm open up beneath her and she put a hand out to Mike to steady herself.

Mike held her by the arm.

"He heard in town that the gypsies have an American in their camp."

Sarah clapped her hand to her mouth and squeezed her eyes shut.

Alive. David was alive.

"I'm glad for you, Sarah. It's good," Mike said carefully. "Well, it could be a little better but, aye, it sounds like he's alive."

Tears seeped out between her fingers and she opened her eyes to look at him.

"Thank you, God," she whispered. "I knew he was okay."

"Well, *that* we do not know, and let's not be getting ahead of ourselves but aye, it gives us something to go on." Mike rubbed her arm lightly where he held her. "And unfortunately I know this means, more than ever, that you won't change your plans to stay." He looked at her sadly.

Sarah wiped her tears away with her fingers and took a deep breath. She smiled briefly, fiercely, at Mike and shook her head.

"You're wrong, Mike," she said. "This changes everything."

"You mean you'll not be insisting on waiting for them brigands to descend upon us?" he said, with hope in his voice.

"No way."

Sarah jumped to her feet. "We're going after the bastards."

THREE HOURS LATER, the young gypsy boy, Conor, slipped silently down from the tall pine that hung over the little encampment and picked his way through the woods past the two sleeping men on guard duty. It had taken all of his self-control not to leave earlier, so excited was he to tell Finn what he'd overheard.

The American woman and her group were planning to raid them!

Once he was sure he was out of earshot of the sleeping guards, Conor broke into a full, arm-pumping run back to the gypsy camp.

22

"You're crazy, you know." Mike surveyed the picnic table in front of him. Every firearm and bit of ammunition, except for the ones carried by each man was on the table.

"How much do we have?" Sarah stood next to him and looked at the table. "Is it very much? Is it enough, do you think?"

"No, it's not enough," he said with exasperation. "There are at least thirty of them and only five of us. If each of us had a Gatling gun and automatic weapons too it wouldn't be enough."

John approached the table. He held a large biscuit in one hand stuffed with jam.

"Wow!" he said. "That is a *lot* of guns." He turned to his mother. "You have to let me come, Mom. We need every man. Mr. Donovan said so."

Sarah turned and looked at Mike.

"I did *not* say the boy should come," Mike said loudly, turning and frowning at John. "I did not say that."

"No, but I know we're outnumbered and we need every man."

"Stop it right now, John," Sarah said. "The answer is no so

please let Mr. Donovan and me continue without having to fight this battle, too."

John blushed and turned away from the table. Sarah called after him but he kept walking.

"Damn it," she said. "I know he's just trying to help..."

"All right," Mike said gruffly. "Here's my plan and you'll abide by it, aye?"

"Of course."

"Oh, don't say that when you know it's the last thing you'll do."

"I don't know what you mean," Sarah said. "I have no idea as to the best way to handle any of this and I'm only too happy to be told what to do."

"Even if, like with young John, I tell you to stay back at camp?"

"Except that."

Mike gave her a withering *I-told-you-so*-look.

"Come on, Mike. The plan?"

Mike looked down at the guns and sighed.

"I'm in the lead," he said, glaring at her as if expecting her to challenge it. "And we'll put two of our lads in the trees the night before."

Sarah nodded. "Snipers?"

"More for coverage, like, than snipers. So when we retreat we don't get all shot to shit."

"That doesn't sound like a great plan," Sarah said, frowning. "In fact, it sounds like planned suicide."

"Which is what I've been telling you all along. Plus..." Mike nodded at the grey skies with scudding dark clouds bunching up on the horizon, "there's a storm coming."

"The Irish aren't afraid of a little bad weather," Sarah said.

"Don't do that,"

"Do what?"

"Pull that national shite on me. Try to make it seem like it's somehow the patriotic thing to do to march into a well-armed camp where we are hopelessly outnumbered. This is not bloody England, you know. We don't buy into that stupid "we the five hundred" shite."

"Six hundred,"

"Okay, how every many hundred, it doesn't matter. This is not an epic poem. This is real life and you are putting every man and his family at risk by this barking mad, crazy…"

"Look, Mike, much as I like to argue this same issue with you over and over again *ad nauseum* let me remind you that I am not the bad guy here. Okay? It's easy to lash out at me for doing what needs to be done, but you know it's *Finn* and his gang who are putting your people at risk, not me." She held up a hand to cut off his protests. "If you think I'm the bad guy then back off right now and I'll go alone."

"I have no doubt you would."

"I would."

"Because you're crazy."

"Because. I. Want. My. Husband. Back."

Mike sighed looked away.

"Look, Mike, let me put it to you this way: if you had a wife, let's say, oh, I don't know, say she's the mother of your children and you love her very much and if she were being held by murdering scum, would you just sit tight, and hope they don't come bother you? Or would you gather up your guns and as many people as you could and go bloody *get* her?"

He shook his head but she could see he finally agreed.

"We're all going to get bloody killed," he said.

"Right," she said, patting him on the shoulder. "Leave the pep talk with the men to me, okay?"

∼

FINN HAD SLEPT VERY WELL. The farmer's bed was soft and large and the fleeing family had been kind enough to leave the linens on the bed. Finn had drunk long into the night but, as usual, woke up refreshed with no ill affects from the night's abuses. It also seemed to him that his bad arm hadn't hurt last night. He massaged it gently. It surprised him to realize that he associated the pain of his healed wound with the continued life of the woman who had caused it. He really believed it would stop hurting him as soon as she was dead. He stood up and looked out the window at the misting Irish morning. Today seemed to be a perfect day for that, he thought with a smile.

DAVID WATCHED the young boy wolfing down a full breakfast over the campfire. He had been present last night when the boy presented his report to Finn. The cheering and the drinking had shifted into high gear at the prospect of a battle with the American and her group. David was as near to a state of shock as could be possible without having taken an actual hit on the head. Up to this moment, he thought Sarah and John were living quietly in the little cottage just as he'd left them. The boy, Conor's, revelation and subsequent speech by Finn destroyed that scenario in one swift, blinding moment.

"THE BITCH IS COMING TO US!" Finn roared to his men. Sparks from the outdoor fire shot into the air almost as if conjured up by him and his words. With a bottle of wine in one hand and a fist in the other, Finn gathered his crew of twenty men. "And we'll meet her halfway. Are we not accommodating?" His gang laughed.

"Remember, I don't want her touched so be mindful of that," he said. "Anyone else with her ye can kill straightaway. D'ya ken?"

He turned and clapped young Conor on the shoulder and handed him the wine bottle. Before he turned to go back into the house where he would drink alone until he passed out, his glance fell briefly on David.

DAVID'S PLAN was easy if not foolproof.

He ate a piece of moldy soda bread and washed it down with cold tea. He felt lucky there was anything to eat this morning at all. Like the others, Brendan had drunk too much and was still asleep. One of the younger gypsy boys, with terrible acne and crossed eyes, had made him breakfast, such as it was. The cold had been awful during the night and David fought now to return feeling to his numb fingers and toes. He slept by the campfire which usually went out a few hours after he nodded off. He wasn't tied or restrained in any way as he was still considered too weak to do much more than bring a spoon back and forth to his lips.

He may have encouraged that belief more than was absolutely accurate.

Most of the gypsies were still sleeping off last night's drinking. Even Finn, usually an early riser, hadn't shown himself yet this morning.

All David had to do was get up as if he were going to relieve himself in the woods, like he had done many times before, and just keep walking. With any luck at all, he'd intercept Sarah and her group well before they were ambushed by Finn's death squad.

He took one more look around the deserted camp, stood up, brushed the nonexistent crumbs from his meager breakfast off his jeans, and headed for the woods.

∼

SARAH SAT QUIETLY ATOP DAN. The bad weather was definitely moving in and quickly. She looked around at the small group of men, also on horseback, and felt a wave of discouragement.

Couldn't the storm have held off just one more day?

Four men sat their horses and alternately watched her and the skies. One—a big fellow named Bill—would stay behind to protect the women and children.

It wasn't early. Sarah hadn't been sure if that mattered and Donovan didn't seem to have an opinion on it.

"D'ya think I have experience in this sort of thing?" he'd responded when she'd queried him.

No one had experience in any of the things they were lately being called upon to do, Sarah thought, least of all her.

She glanced at the black hulk that was once their cottage. Just thinking about Dierdre and the loss of her was enough to make Sarah want to slide out of her saddle and return to her cold bedroll in the barn. The feisty little Irishwoman had been Sarah's emotional mainstay since the crisis had happened. Whether it had been leek and kidney pies or tips on carding wool or common sense advice on how to keep her worries about John's safety at bay, Sarah didn't feel she'd ever find a dearer or more valuable friend.

While the men checked and rechecked their tack and guns and studied the weather, Sarah closed her eyes and prayed.

THE FURTHER HE got from camp, the harder David ran, unmindful of the noise he was making as he crashed through the dense woods. From what he'd heard last night around the campfire, he was fairly certain he knew the direction that Sarah's group was coming. If they were on horseback, they'd have to come down either the main road or across the pastures. Because he didn't know the area or the trails, David ran parallel to the main road.

His arm, mended but not strong, hung at an unnatural angle to his body as he ran.

His mind raced.

Would he be able to hear Sarah's group on the road? Would he be able to identify them? It didn't make sense that Sarah would actually be with them but Finn seemed convinced she would be. Would they shoot first when he hailed them?

Would this nightmare ever be over?

He stumbled against a root and barely caught himself from plowing face first into the ground. His breathing was coming in short, ragged gasps but he was afraid to stop and rest. He needed to get distance from himself and the camp. Even that drunken, lazy crowd had probably noticed his absence by now.

He forced a long breath into his lungs and, exhaling, pushed himself off a small sapling for momentum.

Suddenly David froze. He heard a sound from behind him. Turning, he saw Brendan not twenty paces behind him, his face flushed with exertion.

"Making a run for it, Yank?"

"AND SO, I want to thank each of you," Sarah said, wiping the perspiration from the palms of her hands on her jeans and gripping the reins tightly. "I know that you know we can't live with this group of...of cowards and murderers virtually in our midst and that without any police to protect us, we need to step forward and deal with it."

The men listened passively and for a moment Sarah found herself wondering if they only spoke Gaelic although she knew that wasn't true. Out of the corner of her eye she saw one of the wives standing by the cook fire in jeans and running shoes. The woman stood with her hands on her hips staring directly at Sarah.

It was not a friendly stare.

Why *were* they doing this? She looked at Donovan who was watching the storm clouds move in. *Were they really risking their lives just because Mike asked them to?*

The night before she told herself she didn't care why the men came with her, as long as they did. She would worry about morals and why and all that once she had David back with her. In fact, now that she thought about it she realized that, once David was back, she wouldn't need to think about it.

Unless...she looked at the glowering wife again. Unless some of them didn't come back. Was she asking this woman to risk her husband so that Sarah could retrieve her own? Was this just another case of the rich American's wants trumping everyone else's? Why were these thoughts invading her head now of all times?

In exasperation, Sarah jerked Dan's head away from the center of the camp and pushed him forward with her legs.

I can't think about any of this right now, she thought. *Let's just do this.*

From what Donvoan had told her, she figured it was at least a thirty-minute ride to where the gypsies were camped out at an abandoned neighboring farm. Sarah didn't want to lose the one advantage they had—the surprise factor—and so she'd suggested to Donovan that they not ride in a group but spaced-out in single file. He seemed fine with the suggestion.

She was grateful for him. He was a natural leader and the men in the camp—even the older ones—clearly all looked to him to tell them what to do in this new and uncertain world after the crisis.

As she led Dan out of the camp, she caught John's eye as he stood next to the little cart pony Ned. He waved to her but didn't smile. She had hugged him fiercely not five minutes before she mounted up. Leaving him again left her with a sick feeling and she had to remind herself, nearly by the minute, that what she was doing—as unnatural as it felt—was in fact bringing her family back together again. She waved to him and forced a smile.

Dear God, please don't let this be the last time I see him.

DAVID STARED at the rope winding tighter and tighter around his wrists. He felt like the wind had been knocked out of him but, except to bind his hands, Brendan hadn't touched him. The sickening feeling of being so close in his mind to ending this nightmare and then landing right back in it made him want to vomit.

"Sorry to ruin your plans for the day, mate," Brendan said jovially as he cinched the hemp handcuffs tighter. "Finn thought you might try something like this, today of all days, you know? Not that I appreciate being awakened by a bucket of piss being thrown on me. That's thanks to you."

David looked at the man. "Sorry about that," he said with as much sarcasm as he could muster.

"Do I look worried?" Brendan said, giving the lead rope attached to David's hands a hard yank to test its security. "Now, I may smell a little raw..." He laughed heartily at his own joke and then indicated the path back to camp.

"You don't have to do this," David found himself saying. "You don't have to do everything that sociopath tells you to do, Brendan."

"Feet moving, if you please, Yank," Brendan said, tugging on the lead rope. "I'll drag you behind me all the way if I have to but neither of us'll be happy about it."

"He threw a bucket of piss on you, you said." David began to move in the direction of the camp. "Why would you willingly be his house slave?"

"Unlike yourself, we don't have slaves in Ireland," Brendan said.

"Clearly, you do," David said. "I'm talking to one now."

"Aw, shite, I was hoping we could stay friends a little longer. Name calling me isn't a way to do that."

"Neither is tying up people, Brendan." David held up his hands to illustrate the point.

"Guess that means we're not really friends."

Because Sarah had been thinking of John when she heard the shout, the first thing that came, irrationally, to her mind, was that he had somehow gotten hurt in the brief moments since she had last seen him. She had ridden to the perimeter of the west wall that surrounded the little farm, but she wheeled her horse around and cantered back to the forecourt, looking frantically for the sight of her son.

What she saw, instead, was bad. All three of the men in the group were dismounted and huddled around a form on the ground. Sarah stayed mounted, the better to get a view of what had happened now that she knew it didn't involve John. Donovan's horse was running wildly back and forth in the open paddock, his reins streaming in front of him with each pounding step a threat to become entangled in them.

"What happened?" she yelled to the group. She could see now it was Donovan on the ground.

He wasn't moving.

23

Can this really be happening?

Sarah sat on a hay bale, cupping a tin of piping hot milkless tea. Donovan's horse had spooked nearly an hour earlier leaving him with a broken arm and the raiding party drinking tea by a quickly waning breakfast fire. Sarah had to admit the tea tasted good against the bad day. The storm clouds, while still threatening, had held off their rain so far. John sat next to her. He seemed to be watching her.

"You okay, Mom?"

She reached over and gave his knee a squeeze.

"Of course, sweetie," she said. "Just a little wound up, I guess, because of what happened to Mr. Donovan."

"But you're still going, right?" He looked at her anxiously.

"Yes, John," she said. "Dad's there and so I'm still going."

"Is it...will it be more dangerous without Mr. Donovan?"

Sarah could see his problem. He desperately wanted his dad back but the odds of losing his Mother too just went up significantly. And yet, to do nothing...

"It would be better with him, of course," Sarah said. "But being sneaky will make up for the lack of numbers, I think."

"You're not taking this theory about being sneaky from some television show, are you?" He frowned at her. "'Coz I'm almost positive the writers didn't get their information from first-hand experience, you know?" John shook his head and looked at her. "I'm worried, Mom. You don't seem to have a plan and now with Mr. Donovan out of the picture..."

"I have a plan," Sarah said, tossing the dregs of her tea into the dirt behind her. "Who says I don't have a plan?"

"Really?" The relief in his face buoyed her even though she knew, intellectually, that it was relief based on a hope that had no basis in fact.

She leaned over and hugged him.

"It's all going to work out, sweetheart," she said. "It is."

It is because it has to, she thought.

"Missus?"

Sarah let John go and looked up at Gavin standing before her.

"Me Da says he'd like to talk to you before we head out, if that's okay."

"Is he in much pain?" Sarah got to her feet and, with a brief parting smile to John, followed Gavin into the barn.

"I guess so," he said. "Kinda hard to tell, him being so cheesed off the best of times."

Sarah let her eyes adjust to the darkened barn interior. Gavin took his fully tacked horse out of the one of the stalls and led it outside. Donovan was lying in one of the empty stalls, hay piled around him. Fiona walked out of the stall carrying two empty tea mugs. Sarah assumed they must have just finished a long chat.

Fiona smiled at her as she passed.

"He's not happy, you'll be knowing that straightaway, aye?"

Sarah nodded and returned her smile. She entered the stall and saw Donovan propped up against the far corner. His arm was in a sling but whether anyone in the camp had known enough to set the bone, she didn't know and decided against asking him. His eyes were closed. She came in quietly and knelt down in front of him.

"Hey, Mike," she said softly. "How you doing?"

Stupid question of course.

His eyes opened and the peace she thought she saw in his face when they were closed vanished. A grimace of pain shot across his features.

"I assume you're still going," he said.

"Nothing's really changed," she said. "Except, maybe, our odds."

Donovan looked at her fiercely and spoke in a low voice.

"Put Gavin and Aidan in trees when you get to the camp, yeah?"

"Trees. Right."

"They're the best shots. And they're the ones with the rifles. They can keep the camp pinned down or at least hiding in the house. Gypsies are famous cowards."

"Cowards. Got it."

"Don't be thinking you can waltz into the camp and *parlez* or some such stupid thing, eh?" Donovan glowered at her. "This isn't a movie. If you show yourself, you'll be shot. If not by Finn then by one of his gobshites wanting to show off for him."

"Don't show myself. Right." Sarah nodded and watched him with concern. She knew he was in pain and they had nothing, not even aspirin. It made her think about what other kinds of first aid they might need by the end of the day.

"So," she said. "I got two of my guys in trees, that leaves me and..."

"Jimmy."

"Jimmy." She nodded. "I don't show myself...so, how do I..?"

"Once Gavin and Aidan are in place, they should be able to take out at least a dozen. All hell will break loose in the camp as the bastards try to find out where the shots are coming from and where to hide."

"Then I make my move," she said.

Donovan nodded tiredly.

"I suggest you keep Jimmy back to help as he sees the need and where and, if things go bad, to come back and warn us."

"I see. Yes, that's sensible. You haven't come to my part, yet."

Donovan looked at her.

"Does he know how much you love him?" he asked. "Would he do this for you, do you think?"

Sarah sighed and picked up Donovan's uninjured hand.

"If there's a future for me and David in this life," she said, "I intend to make sure he knows how much he means to me. In my world back home, who he and I were as a couple kind of got lost, you know?"

Donovan just listened, his eyes never leaving her face. "We started out as I guess most people madly in love do. We had dreams of the kind of life we would make for ourselves and any kids we had. And it seems impossible to believe right now, the way I feel and the way the world looks to me now, but somewhere along the way he and I lost touch. Somewhere between all the running around we did to keep John's life on track, school and sports and such, and our own jobs which seemed so important back then, we started going through the motions with each other. It's hard for me to believe that the thing I now see as the most important thing in my life was the thing that got pushed into the background noise of the life I was making."

Donovan just watched her, pain etched on every line in his face.

"So," Sarah said. "My part."

Donovan took a moment to speak. Finally, he said: "When the moment comes where all hell breaks loose, you get into the thick of things. Walk right into the midst of all of 'em yelling and running and shooting, ya understand?"

Sarah nodded.

"Have your guns out—one in each hand. Be ready to use them. You hear me?"

Sarah nodded again.

"I mean it, Sarah. Be ready to shoot anybody who looks at you, let alone tries to stop you. Can you do that?"

"I'm prepared to shoot every person in that camp if I have to," she said.

"There'll be kids there," he said in a warning tone. "So you know. Kids the age of young John there."

That information made her start. He noticed her eyes left his for a minute.

"And every one of the little gobshites would kill you as soon as spit on ya. They're not with Finn against their will, ye ken?"

"I do." Sarah visibly shook herself and the image of shooting children from her head. "So what is my purpose in coming into the camp? To find David?"

"Wrong. To find Finn."

Sarah frowned. "But I…"

"I know what you want, Sarah," Donovan said. "God, I wish I were going with you. Can I not talk you into delaying this insane idea?"

"I find Finn," Sarah said, her stare as hard as diamonds.

"And you kill 'im," Donovan said simply before sagging back against the wall, the energy of his statement sapping what strength he had left. "*Don't* talk with him, don't ask him questions, don't tell him why, just shoot the bastard. You got that?"

Sarah stood up. "Shoot the bastard. Got it."

"The rest of 'em won't fight on without the head of the snake. You may still need to shoot a few more, mind, if they don't know Finn's dead. But once they do, things should settle down pretty quick."

"Okay, thanks, Mike," Sarah said. "I've waited longer than I wanted to and need to get going. Thank you."

He nodded at her. "Be careful, Sarah," he said. "Come back safe to your lad."

Sarah nodded grimly.

"Take care of yourself, Mike," she said, then turned and left.

FINN DIVIDED ten of his men to stand on either side of the main road. He had already sent another dozen down the road to meet the American and her party. While they only had hunting rifles and knives, it would be enough. The sun had been directly up in the sky for more than an hour and Finn was beginning to worry about why the ambush hadn't taken place yet. He'd sent them out hours ago. His gaze sought out the young boy, Conor, who had brought him the information the night before. He watched him throw a stick to a camp dog then turn and urinate against one of the farmer's dead rose bushes. He'd pranced around last night like some kind of hero, telling and retelling about his run from the American's camp. If the American bitch didn't come after all, he'd butcher the kid and throw his pox-infested body into the rose bushes. Wouldn't hurt to remind the rest of 'em who was in charge.

Standing in the front yard of the little farmhouse, Finn would be able to see the first hint of anyone coming down the front drive from the main road. His men stood flanking the main road for nearly two hours now. Most of them were sitting, some of them were lying down asleep. Finn's anxiety began to throb in his chest like a panicked bird.

Maybe the American knew Conor was listening? Maybe she was setting him up?

Plus, the American bastard and Brendan were still not back. As soon as he formed the thought in his head he realized that this was, largely, the core of his agitation. He needed her husband for this plan for torturing the bitch to work.

GAVIN INSISTED on being in the lead. Sarah guessed it might have something to do with an order from his father so she tucked in behind him and kept Dan at a slow trot. The posting action of rising up and down actually helped dissipate the anxious energy that was coursing through her.

Every time she rose out of the saddle, her stomach muscles clenched and then released and the action began to calm her, like being forced to take deep inhalations and exhale. Sarah imagined what men going to battle on horseback for hundreds of years must have felt like. They must have taken comfort from the rhythm and familiarity of the horse beneath them, just like she was doing, even as it carried them closer and closer to probable death.

Aidan and Jimmy rode behind her. All of a sudden, it struck Sarah how foolish this plan was. Unless they were going to talk with the gypsies—which they were not—they couldn't hope to penetrate their camp and kill their leader without being killed themselves.

Is John right? Have I been watching too many action movies? Is there any way this can have a happy ending?

At the very moment Sarah was a breath away from calling to Gavin to tell him to turn back, she heard the gunshot.

As if in slow-motion, she watched Gavin grunt and then drop from the saddle, his hands clawing at his horse as he fell.

24

Davistol jogged carefully through the underbrush in the woods that surrounded the pastures in the direction that Brendan had indicated. He knew a wrong step in a hidden pothole would be the end of him and his hopes of finding Sarah in time.

When he heard the gunshot, he stopped. Brendan had warned him not to but he stood, undecided, on the verge of the pasture. He had seen no traffic of any kind on the road, not horses, not pedestrians.

What could the gunshot mean?

He looked back over his shoulder. It was totally quiet. Only the sound of his own labored breathing broke the silence.

He'd known from the minute that Brendan found him that he wasn't serious about bringing him back to camp. He was too slow, too interested in talking. It hadn't taken much to make the promises that bought David's freedom.

"I'll give you more money than you'll see in a lifetime," David had said.

"Five thousand US," Brendan said. He'd obviously given it some thought.

David nearly laughed in his face. *Why not make it a million? he thought.*

"Done," he said.

"I know the Yanks'll come for your lot sooner or later," Brendan said. "This is money in the bank for me, so it is."

"Smart move, Brendan. Alive, I can make you a rich man," David had said, holding his bound hands out for the big gypsy to cut. "Dead, I'm just another blot in that big copybook in the sky."

It had been exactly the right thing to say. The big gypsy was clearly not feeling too secure about where he stood with God these days. It made complete sense to him that God's way would also make him rich.

Brendan gave David directions back to his cottage—except the cottage was not where David was going.

Now he turned in the direction of the gunshot and prayed like he had never prayed before.

WHEN DAN REARED UP, Sarah didn't have time to lean forward. She tumbled to the ground and immediately felt rough hands on her, pulling her away from the horse's feet. Both knees of her jeans ripped in the fall and she bloodied her elbow, too.

A man grabbed her and more men scrambled from out of the bushes by the side of the road, reaching for her, and her horse. She twisted in their grips and saw the still form of Gavin crumpled in the middle of the road. Her stomach lurched and she vomited on the man who held her the tightest.

"Blimey! The bitch puked on me!"

"Shut your gob, you git! Just bring 'er."

Sarah tried to wrench free from the two men. They were wiry and muscled.

Even terrified and sickened, Sarah found herself turning away from the sour breath of the one closest to her. He kept his face near hers as if, any moment, he would lean over and take a bite out of her.

"The bastards are getting away!" the gypsies yelled.

Sarah heard more gunshots and prayed that Jimmy and Aidan had the sense to get off the main road as they retreated. Her eyes rested on Gavin.

That's my fault, she thought. *I did that. To Mike's boy...*

"Forget it. They're too far away."

"Should we go after 'em?"

"Nah. Let's get these two back to camp. He was expectin' 'em hours ago."

They were bringing Gavin, too? Did that mean he was still alive?

One of the two men let go of Sarah's arm long enough to tie her hands in front of her. They pushed her towards a small horse. They ignored Gavin.

She heard one of the men behind her rasp out sharply:

"Let's go, boyo. Try to run and we shoot yer mum, eh?"

Sarah snapped her head around, nearly jerking herself out of the vice-grip of her captor.

Twenty yards away, John sat on his pony, the reins looped in the hands of a tall skinny youth who was leading him down the road.

Sarah gasped.

"Finn'll be pleased," one of the men said as he roughly turned her to face the horse and boosted her into the saddle. "We're bringin' him a little bonus."

The howls of laughter from the men echoed in Sarah's ears as they rode down the road, each horse carefully stepping over or around poor Gavin.

~

"What do you mean you couldn't find him?" Finn said.

Brendan rubbed his hands along his jeans and looked at his feet. He had returned ten minutes ago, empty handed.

Finn glanced around the nearly deserted camp, his frustration coming off him in waves. He looked back at Brendan standing before him.

"You let the bastard go," he said, biting off every word.

Brendan looked at his leader. "No," he said.

"You did."

"I tell ye, I couldn't find 'im."

"What did he promise you?" Finn stuck his face close to Brendan's and the man recoiled. "Money? American dollars? An hour with his wife?"

"I didn't find 'im, Mack. I swear."

"I need that bastard back here!" Finn shrieked. "They're bringing his wife down that road any minute."

"Maybe I...I could try again, aye?" Perspiration from Brendan's scalp began to trickle into his eyes. "I bet I know the way he went."

Finn pulled out a pistol from the waistband at the small of his back. Brendan took two steps back and put his hands up.

"Oh, Jesus, Mack, I can find him. I *will* find him." Brendan's eyes darted from the gun and back to Finn's face.

"You've helped enough, boyo," Finn said and shot him twice in the chest.

David knelt by Gavin's body. His holster was empty. The boy was still breathing but there was nothing David could do for him. It was at least two miles on foot back to the gypsies' camp.

"I'm sorry, son," he said to the unconscious boy. "I've got to leave you." He touched the young man's sleeve and, for a moment, got an image in his head of John laughing at one of the puppies' antics.

David stood up, with no weapon between him and his goal—no gun, no knife—and turned to jog down the main road in the direction of Finn's camp.

SARAH REELED FROM THE SLAP. She had been dragged from her mount the minute they entered the camp. She recognized the gypsy she had shot back in October. He was standing over the body of a man lying in the middle of the courtyard between the barn and the farmhouse.

She heard John yell out in a terrible, broken voice: "Dad!"

Sarah caught her breath and for one sickening, endless moment she too thought the man on the ground was David.

The gypsy leader turned on his heel and walked over to where she stood next to the horse, her hands bound in front of her. His eight men stood around her as if they were presenting her to him. Without a word, he backhanded her, driving her into the dirt.

"Get 'er up," he barked harshly.

Sarah felt rough hands jerk at her jacket, and pull her back to a standing position. Her legs buckled and one of the men grabbed her under her arm and kept her standing.

"Hey, Mack, we brung ya two for the price of one."

The men laughed and it was all Sarah could do not to throw up again.

My precious child. Dear God, don't let this be happening.

Finn turned from Sarah and looked in the direction his men were pointing. Sarah saw his face relax.

"Well, I'll be banjaxed," he said.

Two of his men dragged John off his pony and over to Finn.

Sarah, her lip bloodied and throbbing, twisted in her captor's hands to put herself between Finn and her boy.

Finn looked at Sarah.

"You'll soon be knowing what it feels like to lose a cherished loved one," he said to her. "I've got your handsome husband, too, you know."

Sarah stared at the gypsy and licked her lips, tasting her own blood. She watched his eyes to see if there was any sanity there at all.

"He's not too handsome at the moment though."

"Mom, you okay?" John's eyes were wide with fear. Sarah couldn't imagine what she must look like to him. "You leave her alone!"

The gypsy holding him gave his jacket a hard jerk.

"Shirrup, ya hear?"

John never took his eyes off his mother.

Oh, my God, she thought, her stomach roiling. *He thinks I have a plan.*

"Take 'em both into the house," Finn said. "I got a little surprise I need to get ready." He gestured to the body on the ground. "Somebody move this piece of shite before I trip over it."

The men took Sarah and John into one of the bedrooms in the farmhouse. One of them tied John's hands in front of him then shoved the boy onto the bed and walked out.

Sarah heard him say to the other gypsy as he left: "Arseways bastard coulda said good work or something."

John scrambled to his feet and ran to Sarah.

"Mom, I'm sorry. I thought...when Mr. Donovan got hurt, I thought...I just wanted to..."

"It's okay, sweetie. It's okay."

"What are we gonna do?" He looked around the room. The bedroom had a window facing the back of the farm. Sarah sat on the bed, her knees no longer able to support her. She had screwed this up badly. She tried to banish the nausea and self-recrimination long enough to think. She tried to steady herself with deep breaths.

"You okay, Mom?" John sat down on the bed next to her. "You're breathing funny."

"I'm good, sweetheart. Did he hurt you when he tied your hands?" Just saying the words out loud made her want to break down and cry.

"They're not even really tied," John said pulling his hands out of the bind. "See? The cord's too big so he couldn't make a good knot."

"You...you didn't bring a gun, did you?"

"No, you told me I'm not allowed to have a gun."

"Yes, that's right. That's right."

"I coulda, though, Mom. They didn't even check me for weapons. Guess they figured I don't count. So they didn't find this." John rolled up his pant leg and pulled out a small knife from his sock.

Sarah took another deep breath.

"That's good, sweetie. Hide it someplace easier to get to than your sock, okay?"

"Don't you want me to cut you loose?"

"Yeah, good idea." She held out her hands. "Don't worry about nicking me. Just pay attention to any sounds of someone coming."

John began to saw through the rope when they heard foot-steps outside.

"Hide it," Sarah whispered, pulling her hands back.

The footsteps headed to the kitchen and then out the front door.

"I can't believe they're just leaving us here," Sarah said.

"You can bet there's a guard on the front door, though," John said, resuming his work on her cord.

Another noise made them both freeze. This time the noise came from outside the back window.

"Guards out back too, I guess?" Sarah said, trying not to let the words sap all her energy for whatever lay ahead.

John went to the window and pulled back the curtain to peer out. Suddenly he dropped his knife and yelped. Hands reached into the window and grabbed him.

25

D avid clapped his hand over John's mouth praying Sarah wouldn't start yelling too. He pulled himself into the room, not letting go of John. He had listened long enough out the window to know they were alone. But they wouldn't be for long if Sarah screamed.

Sarah stood by the bed, her eyes huge, both her hands covering her mouth. David held John to him and took the two steps to Sarah to gather her into his arms as well.

"Oh, my God," Sarah whispered into his chest as his arms closed around her.

John hugged his father fiercely.

David pulled away and looked into his wife's eyes. Her face was bruised and bloodied.

"We need to go, family," he said. "Out the window and fast before they come back to check on you."

Sarah nodded, looking at her husband. "You're really here."

"John, you go first," David said, pushing the boy toward the window. "It's a five foot drop. Clear the bushes and wait for us. Go."

Before John could turn for the window the door swung open.

Mack Finn was framed in the doorway.

"Well, well. This is even better than the surprise I had planned," he said, his eyes going from John to Sarah and David. He held a small machete with a large sawback blade loosely in his hand. The butt of Sarah's semi-automatic protruded obscenely from the front waistband of his trousers.

"Don't try it, boyo," he said to John. He stepped into the room with two men behind him, both armed with rifles. Finn leaned over and scooped up the dropped knife at his feet.

"Now this is interesting," Finn said, looking at the knife. "Yours?" He gestured to John.

"Leave him alone, Finn," David snarled.

Finn turned back to him.

"Or what, Yank? Did you see your mate, Brendan? I left him out there so you could see what you did to him."

"You left him out there so the rest of your scum could see what happens to people who cross you," David said, moving in front of Sarah.

"Tie 'im," Finn said. One of his men put his gun down and fastened David's hands behind his back. When he was finished, he picked up his gun and smashed the butt of it into David's face. Sarah screamed and grabbed for David as he sank to his knees.

"You...you bastard!" John screamed, his hands clenched in fists of fury and frustration.

Finn hefted his knife in his hands.

"You remember me?" He spoke to Sarah. "You remember me coming to your place and you shooting me and me brother? You remember?"

Sarah stared at the gypsy and willed herself not to look at John or David. Somehow, she knew that calling attention to how much they meant to her would not be a good move right now.

"I remember you," she said. "You tried to steal my horses. Your brother was hurting my boy."

Finn was shaking his head.

"No, no, no! That is *not* what happened. We were hungry, so we were, and we came upon your place and begged for food."

"That's not how I remember it," Sarah said. Out of the corner of her eye she saw John fidgeting. She wanted to reassure him. Her whole body ached to tell him everything would be okay. But she knew not only that the words were a lie but the trigger by which this madman would use to end all their lives.

"Do you remember this?" Finn wrenched his shirt away from his shoulder to reveal an angry red mark the size of a tangerine, puckered around the edges on his upper arm. He covered himself with a jerk, as if suddenly embarrassed to have shown so much. He held the knife to Sarah's chin.

"If the brat moves, shoot him," he said over his shoulder.

Suddenly, Finn reached down and grabbed David by the shirtfront and jerked him to his feet. With his hands behind him, David was defenseless but he met the gypsy's stare.

"Bet you live in a big mansion back in America, huh?" Finn spoke with his face inches from David's. "Bet you have three cars, don't you?"

David stared at him. "Go to hell," he said.

Finn flushed angrily. "Hold 'im," he said. The same man who had hit David set his gun aside and held David from behind.

Sarah tried to put herself between David and Finn.

"Please, don't," she said before Finn checked her hard in the jaw with his elbow. Blood gushed out of her mouth and she collapsed to a sitting position on the bed.

"Mom!" The anguish in John's voice brought Sarah out of the daze of pain that clouded her head. She looked up and saw Finn position his knife against David's chest and then draw it slowly from one side to the other, through his thin jacket and the soiled tee shirt beneath it. Blood blossomed in crimson blots in the knife's trail.

Sarah heard David moan loudly at the same time she saw the blur of brown and blue as John launched himself onto Finn's back in a flurry of fists and kicks. She heard Finn's grunt of surprise and saw him reach up to dislodge the boy from his back, his hand still holding the knife dripping with David's blood.

The Glock in Finn's waistband was eye level with her where she sat. She wrapped her fingers around the handle and without bothering to pull it free from his trousers fired three rounds.

Finn screamed and jerked convulsively. She wrenched the gun out as he fell, his knife clattering to the floor ahead of him... and shot the armed man in the doorway. She turned her attention to the gypsy holding David and pointed the gun at him.

"No, missus!" the gypsy cried, looking at his rifle as he spoke and clearly gauging his chances of reaching it.

John scrambled off Finn's thrashing body and grabbed up the rifle. He picked up the dead gypsy's gun too and then turned back to Finn and fished the knife out from under his twitching body. He stood there, panting, holding the two rifles and the knife in his arms as if trying to remember something.

"Untie him," Sarah said to the gypsy near David. The man nodded vigorously and quickly untied David who put his hands to his bleeding chest. "John, give your Dad some of that bedding and help him press it against his wound. David, you look like you're going to pass out. Are you?" David collapsed into a sitting position onto the bed.

"I'll live," he said hoarsely. "Is he dead?"

She kept the muzzle of her gun pointed in the direction of the remaining gypsy.

"Check him," she said.

He held his hands up and stepped over to Finn's body, now quiet. He knelt down, listened to his chest, and then looked up at Sarah.

"Dead as a cod," he said.

"John, see if the door will lock," Sarah said. "You," she said to the gypsy.

"Name's Mick."

"I don't care what your name is. Move to the front door. Don't touch the doorknob."

They could hear loud voices outside the bedroom door.

"Finn? You okay in there?"

"I'm not gonna hurt you, missus," Mick said, grinning at her.

Why was the bastard smiling at her? Sarah wondered. *Were they all demented?*

John sat on the bed where his father was lying and held a folded up sheet to his wound. The collected rifles and the knife were in a pile at his feet.

Sarah stood in front of the back window.

"You are going to tell anyone outside that door to back off," she said to him. "You are going to tell them—"

"Mom, look out!

Sarah heard the noise behind her and instinctively turned toward it. Out of the corner of her eye she could see Mick moving fast in her direction but she could only deal with what was in front of her—a large, bearded man pointing a shotgun at her from the window.

Sarah dove to the floor while firing blindly at him, three, four, rounds. The man took two in the chest that she could see before his gun clattered to the bedroom floor and he fell back outside.

She heard John yell out: "You got 'im! You got 'im!" and she turned to see the gypsy, Mick, lying not six inches from where she was, two bullet holes in his head—and John's knife in his hand. She looked up and saw David sitting on the bed, a gun in his hand.

Sarah put her empty gun down and wrapped her arms around her husband and son.

"Come on, Mom," John said, standing up. "We can't quit now. There's about a hundred gypsies out there."

"David, how are you doing?" Sarah asked. She touched the blood soaked pad he was holding to his chest.

"It hurts like shit," he said. "But I don't think anything major got cut. John's right," he said, nodding at the back window. "We're not home yet."

"I know, I know." Sarah picked up a rifle, cracked it open to check it was loaded and stood up. "This back bedroom is not safe. We can't see what's going on. We need to get away from that window."

"Oy! Mrs. Woodson!" A voice called from the back window. "Don't shoot, missus! It's me, Aidan."

Sarah looked at David, her mouth open in astonishment. John ran to the back window before Sarah could stop him.

"Aidan, hey, it's me, John! What are you doing here?"

"Oy, John, Mike says to tell your mum not to shoot him. We're here to save ya!"

26

S

arah sat on the front porch steps of Dierdre and Seamus's cottage. A month had passed since the killings at the gypsy camp. Since then, Sarah and David and John had left their burnt out rental cottage and moved into the McClenny's farm. They brought their horses, Rocky and Dan and the two ponies with them. The pony trap sat on the side of the barn. When the snows melted, they would all learn how to drive it.

It was only March, with plans for planting Dierdre's garden still weeks away, but the larder was full of the food that the gypsies had stolen and stacked in boxes in a barn. Sarah felt guilty every time she pulled out a can or one of the stolen boxes but David brushed away her concerns.

"The people they stole that food from are long gone," he told her.

"One way or the other," John added ominously.

The boy was so much older than his eleven years, Sarah thought.

When Mike had come charging into the gypsy camp, he had no way of knowing that Finn was dead. He rode in, his arm in a sling, Aidan and Jimmy behind him and Fiona and two plucky and pissed-off wives behind them. Mike told Sarah later that he believed that the two women—Janie and Shannon—would've set fire to the place if he hadn't talked them out of it, so angered were they by what they'd done to poor Gavin.

Gavin survived his wound, which turned out to be a bullet to the shoulder, straight in and straight out. "The easiest he could have hoped for," Mike said over and over again to Gavin's extreme annoyance. Aidan and Jimmy had circled around and gone back for him as soon as it was safe to do so.

Mike, Gavin and his group settled into a makeshift community within two miles of where Sarah and David now lived. She rode over to visit with Fiona at least once a week and often more. In all her life she'd never felt more connected to another woman than she did with Fi. Together they talked about men, food preparation, and how the world looked to them now. In the space of one short month, Fiona had become the sister Sarah never had.

She was glad to see that David and Mike seemed to have become friends. She felt she owed a large debt to the big Irishman. He had risked a lot for her family and she vowed privately that she would never forget it.

Now, she sat on the porch, waiting to see Mike's wagon come up the main driveway to their farm. When he and Gavin visited, they always brought fresh meat with them.

John came around the corner of the house with his dog Patrick at his heels. "Hey, Mom," he said. "Waiting for Uncle Mike?"

Sarah wasn't sure when Mike had been granted family status by John but she liked the sound of it.

"I am. Dinner and biscuits are out of the oven. Where's Dad?"

"Still messing with the fence," he said. "It won't close or something."

How soon we take each other for granted, Sarah thought with a smile. The reunion, once all elements of danger had been removed, had been lengthy and exquisite. Just the sight of David at any odd time of the day was enough to fill Sarah with so much love and gratitude she felt overwhelmed by her happiness.

"You'll freeze out here." David spoke as he followed his son from around the house. He grinned at his wife. He had wire cutters in his hands which were covered by an old pair of Seamus's work gloves he'd found in the barn.

Sarah returned his smile. "I didn't even notice," she said.

"You would if you'd just spent two hours standing in the middle of a pasture trying to fix a gap in the fence. What is it with the Irish and no trees? Hey, Sport, take these into the barn for me, will you?" David handed the wire cutters to John.

"Mom, can I ride before dinner?" John said. His face was flushed from the cold.

"No, sweetie. Mike and Gavin will be here in a minute. In fact, if your chores are done, it's time to wash up. You, too," she said, turning to David. She cupped his cheek with her hand. He still hadn't shaved but the look seemed to suit him and this new rugged life they had. He leaned over and kissed her.

"Yeah, yeah," John said, turning toward the barn. "Come on, Patrick. It just gets worse from here."

David wrapped his arms around Sarah and she let all the tension leave her body.

Sarah caught the sight of Donovan's wagon coming down the driveway.

"Oh! They're here," she said, not immediately moving from her husband's arms.

"Great. Mike was supposed to see if he could do anything with the broken handle on the wood splitter I showed him last time." David turned and waved to the two men in the wagon.

DINNER WAS roast lamb with biscuits and mashed potatoes plus preserved green beans from Dierdre's root cellar. David and Sarah's stash of Côte de Rhône had been destroyed in the fire at the cottage but Mike usually brought poteen or whiskey when he came. Watered down enough, Sarah could just manage to drink it.

After dinner, Gavin and John played chess by the fireplace while the adults smoked and drank at the dining table. Sarah lit candles and kept the cook stove door open so the heat would fill the dining room.

"I still can't believe how he's bounced back," Sarah said, watching Gavin in amazement. "He was shot a little more than a month ago and here he is like it's a sprain or something."

Mike lit his pipe and waved out the match flame. "You'd know it when it comes time to doing any chores," he said, looking over at his son.

"You know, Mike—" Sarah started.

"Sure, if this is another apology for nearly getting me only son killed, then please just stop there, Sarah," Mike said. "Your scones are worth any number of dead or maimed sons, sure they are and I had no idea when I first met you that that would be the case."

David laughed.

"We were all so lucky," Sarah said. "None of us got killed and it could so easily have gone the other way."

David leaned over and took her hand. "But it didn't," he said.

Sarah looked at him and smiled.

Mike cleared his throat. "I've got news," he said.

"I hate it when you say that," Sarah said, gathering dishes to take to the kitchen. "Your news always sucks."

David had been leaning back in his chair but sat up abruptly. "News about the Crisis?"

Mike nodded. He reached into his pocket, pulled out a cell phone and placed it on the dining room table among the serving bowls, ashtrays and whiskey glasses.

David said, "Is that what I think it is?"

John jumped up and ran to the table. "What is it? What is it?" he said. He leaned over and snatched it up. "A cell phone!"

"Aye," Mike said. "That it is."

"Doesn't work," Gavin called from the hearth.

"Well, it *would* work," Mike said. "But its charge has run down."

Sarah returned to the table. "This isn't the news," she said, looking at Mike.

"No, it isn't," Mike agreed.

"God, you two developed a secret language while I was gone," David said. "Should I be jealous?"

"So what is the news?" Sarah asked, ignoring David.

Mike took a sip from his glass of whiskey.

"Come on, Da," Gavin said. "Or I'll tell 'em and I'm not as good a teller as you."

Mike placed his glass on the table. "One of Gavin's mates had gone off, same as poor Craig Cahill did, and he's only just returned. He brought a couple of these back and when they were charged up, they worked fine."

"The grid's back on?" David asked, leaning eagerly over the table toward Mike. "The towers are back up?"

"Nothing near us right now," Mike said, "but there's hope it's starting to come back. This mate of Gavin's says there's rumors that communication in London is restored and there are a few vehicles moving about there too now."

Sarah covered her mouth. *Was it over? Was the nightmare really about to be over?*

"They got cars working again?" David asked.

"They shipped some in from Germany and Italy," Mike said. "This bloke said Dublin's got power on and off and he heard there's activity in Limerick, too." He looked at Sarah. "United States military looks like."

John put the cell phone back onto the table. "So," he said, "we're going home."

Sarah looked at him with surprise at his flat tone. He met her eyes over the table and walked back to where Gavin was sitting.

"I'm thinking the lad's got the right of it," Mike said, looking at Sarah. "You'll likely be leaving soon. Probably don't even need to bother planting. You won't be here for the harvest."

"Wow." David sat back in his chair and crossed his arms. He looked at Sarah and smiled. "That *is* news," he said.

"So I was thinking," Mike said, speaking to David now. "It might make sense for the three of you to come into the community. No sense in making a go of it here. And you'll be safer with us."

Sarah knew David had no intention of moving them into the community—temporarily or not. They'd had a few words about it but, in the end, the agreement had been to let David have his way. Her eyes flickered to Mike as he sat easily in the armchair drinking his whiskey.

In more ways than one, it might be safer for them to stay where they were.

"No, thanks, Mike," David said, moving over to Sarah and draping an arm around her shoulders. "We're just fine here until the US gets off its ass and comes to rescue us."

Sarah watched something pass across Mike's face but it was too fleeting to identify. He leaned over to refill all their glasses although Sarah hadn't taken the first sip from hers.

"So, we'll drink to it, aye?" He held up his glass: "To getting things back to normal. And to the Woodsons getting back home."

"Here, here," David said, drinking.

"Cheers," Sarah said in a whisper, but didn't touch her glass.

WELL, Mom, I haven't written in so long but since you haven't been receiving any of these letters anyway I didn't think you'd mind. LOL. It's now been two months since we fought the gypsies and won and five months since what people around here refer to as "the Crisis."

When we found out last month that rescue might be imminent, it's hard to explain but life actually got harder! Up until then, we relished every little pleasure or luxury we could get—whether it was a hot bath or a real chicken dinner instead of beans but as soon as we heard that this period of our lives was temporary, it seems all we could do was focus on the things we were missing and were waiting for us back home. It's hard to explain.

We've been happy here. I know that sounds bizarre and as I look back over it, I'm kind of surprised, myself. But we have. And honestly, except for missing you and Dad, our lives here have been much richer than anything we had back home. Crazy, huh? No electricity, no cars, no shopping! Doesn't make sense to me, either.

Anyway, I'm beyond hopeful and anxious to see you and Dad again after all this time.

Love, Sarah

~

THREE MONTHS after writing that letter, Sarah stood by the fence behind Deidre and Seamus's cottage and watched John trot his pony toward Mike's community.

The compound was an easy two-mile ride on horseback across the pastures, the way John went, but it was nearer to five by the road—a road already grown over with weeds and bushes after seven months of non-use by automobiles. Sarah always thought the Irish roads were better suited to horses anyway. They wound and twisted in illogical gyrations that seemed to fit a horse's meandering style of travel.

It was four months since they found out that rescue was coming. Four months of letter writing and hoping and waiting.

But no one came.

It had been a hard winter—one in which, because they hadn't planted anything—they needed to rely on food and fellowship from Mike's community. And while it kept them alive, the dependency did little to soften David's growing frustration as the months ticked by and no word of rescue came.

As Sarah watched John disappear from sight across the pasture, knowing he'd be safe once he got to Mike's place, knowing he'd be surrounded by friends and watched over by Mike and Fiona, she wondered for the hundredth time why she and David needed to live so far outside the circle.

But, of course, she knew why.

"Anything in the traps?"

Sarah turned to watch her husband trudge up the hill toward her, his face slack and guarded against hope. It was only September, but already the traps were usually empty, the rabbits having tucked themselves up in their burrows until the Irish weather proved more accommodating.

She pointed to the trap at her feet, the body of the little rabbit ensnared in it.

"Thank God," David said, bending down to pry open the steel jaws.

She looked over his shoulder at the expanse of pasture behind him. It was green for as far as she could see, studded by one or two grazing animals.

"John went to Mike's place," she said. David made a face. She knew he was conflicted about their son spending so much time in the community. But the boy was fed and cared for there—something David and Sarah struggled to do on a daily basis.

"I know. I told him to be back in time for dinner," David said. "And now there'll be something for him to eat when he does."

Sarah glanced at the trap, the spring still bloody, then watched her husband pull out his knife and begin to skin the rabbit. It never ceased to amaze her how much their lives had changed. If you had told her a year ago that David would be able to skin a rabbit without even thinking twice about it...well, she'd never have believed it.

Her gaze strayed again to the tree line at the end of the pasture where she could just make out the smoke of the main cook stoves which always burned at the compound. She wondered what was on the camp menu tonight. Fresh rabbit or not, she wouldn't blame John if he'd rather stay in the camp.

"Oh!" she said suddenly, "I just remembered there's a council meeting tonight. I promised Fi we would come. Do you mind very much? We can bring the rabbit."

David followed the direction of her gaze. "No. As it happens, I have something to say at the meeting."

Sarah frowned. "You do?" She watched his fingers move quickly to strip the skin from the rabbit, turning it before her eyes from a furry woodland creature to a piece of steak ready for the grill.

He stood up and wiped his blade against his jeans. "I didn't want to say anything before but I saw something when I was out riding the western pasture today."

"Saw something? Saw what?" Sarah felt the anxiety creeping into her arms and legs.

"It might be nothing," he said. "I found some cart grooves, like someone came through during the night carrying something heavy in the back. There were a bunch of cigarette butts on the ground, too."

Sarah sucked in a breath. Cigarettes were the first thing everyone ran out of after the bomb dropped.

Everyone around here, any way.

"Is that all?"

He hesitated and Sarah realized he was trying to spare her. After everything they had been through, he was still trying to protect her.

"I found a stuffed animal on the ground. A teddy bear."

When she didn't respond he said, "It had blood on it." He gave Sarah's shoulder a squeeze and turned to head back to the cottage. "I'll get the wagon hitched. Be ready in fifteen."

The wind caught the scent of the wood smoke from Mike's community and sent it wafting toward Sarah. She took two steps toward it before she realized what she was doing.

With the wind came a chill that cut through her jacket and whipped her hair around her face. With mounting panic, she turned and ran toward the cottage.

To SEE what happens next in the Irish End Games saga, be sure to order *Going Gone, Book 2, available everywhere.*

ABOUT THE AUTHOR

USA TODAY Bestselling Author Susan Kiernan-Lewis is the author of *The Maggie Newberry Mysteries,* the post-apocalyptic thriller series *The Irish End Games, The Mia Kazmaroff Mysteries, The Stranded in Provence Mysteries, The Claire Baskerville Mysteries,* and *The Savannah Time Travel Mysteries.*

If you enjoyed *Free Falling,* please leave a review on your purchase site.

Visit www.susankiernanlewis.com or follow Author Susan Kiernan-Lewis on Facebook.